HERMETICA

ALAN LEA

DETRITUS BOOKS
OLYMPIA, WA

Advance praise for

HERMETICA

"Hermetica is a rare book, at once readable and thought-provoking. At once a useful metaphor and entertaining. It sits well among the classics of social science fiction but also says something new, tells a story I've never read before. Alan Lea is a writer to watch. To put it plainly, this book is really fucking good.

—Margaret Killjoy, author of *The Lamb Will Slaughter the Lion*

"A compelling thought experiment about the day after tomorrow and the universe next door, Hermetica offers neither hope nor escape, but instead something more important: preparation."

—Nick Mamatas, author of *The Second Shooter*

"Through the eyes of an unusual, neurodivergent protagonist, Alan Lea creates a meticulously well crafted interstellar society still scarred by a pandemic and a troubled past. A vital story that carves an area uniquely its own in deep space literature, Hermetica is at once a tale for our times, a warning for a future that may be upon us, and a gripping mystery."

—Adi Callai, author of *The Sodomites*

FIRST DETRITUS BOOKS EDITION 2021

Published in the USA by Detritus Books

DETRITUS BOOKS
PO BOX 6171
OLYMPIA, WA 98506
detritusbooks.com

Alan Lea is on Twitter @AlanLea11

Detritus Books ISBN: 978-1948501156

Distributed by AK Press

Printed in Canada

10 9 8 7 6 5 4 3 2

HERMETICA

ALAN LEA

1

IT WAS WHEN DASE FOUND A SHEET OF TREE FIBER inside the wall, stamped with black ink in the likeness of words—words referring to "Earth"—that they realized things did not add up. Why had they pried open the wall panel in their module in the first place? Destruction of one's module was destruction of Hermetica itself, and no behavior was more selfish, more dangerous, than sabotage.

Of course, Snookums had started it, scratching at the panel. Not that that would count as a mitigating factor in any reconciliation process Dase might be invited to join to address the sabotage. Snookums was a cat. A fugitive, almost certainly; inexplicable, at least for the moment; but at the end of the day, a cat; therefore, not a citizen; therefore, not party to reconciliation processes. In fact, the relevant Agreements would probably class Snookums' misdeed as negligent sabotage on Dase's watch. Even though Snookums was not assigned to Dase, did not even appear to be in the system, Dase had permitted the cat into the module, had watched as the cat scratched fervently at the wall, had joined in the destructive enterprise, and now... everything was unraveling at a terrifying speed.

When Dase was younger, they knew they wanted to work on the sky. The day Snookums appeared, the sky was a perfect azure and argent dome. It was oppressive in its glory. Dase wanted to reach out, to touch it, to paint a little wisp of cloud, just there. But they were not allowed. The sky was the domain of others, who had been judged and found more worthy. How summarily unfair that a single exam had reduced Dase to a peon. After staring a moment longer at the exquisite sky, Dase let their head fall, chest to chin, and trudged off down the block.

Dase had dosed that morning, but still they could not summon the will to smile a greeting to the people they passed. The mere thought of this failure brought the tears, a growing weight begging release. A release they could not allow. Some moisture around the rim could fall within the probability shadow of allergies or sleepiness, not likely in their file but still possible. But a whole, fat tear rolling down a cheek would definitely result in Dase getting sent home, marking up another sick day. Which in itself wasn't a problem. Even at 15% productivity, Dase would not be classed for permanent reconciliation unless they also logged a couple antisocials. But it would, ineluctably, feel like another failure. One more in an unbroken train, going as far back as they cared to look, as far forward as they dared to imagine.

Perhaps working on the sky had been an unpragmatically ambitious dream. Designers required the highest aptitudes in aesthetics, mechanics, and maths. They had to be team players. The sky formed a joint project with Engineering, LifeSys, and Meteo. Dase's high aptitudes in intuitive, low scores in teamwork, and fine appreciation for suffering had tracked them into palliative therapy. Yet wasn't that, on another level, an affirmation of their feelings? Dase had the unshakable feeling that it was their destiny to touch the sky. What other dreams could one have, condemned to die in transit? For Dase's cohort, there was no final destination.

Dase's office, like all health centers on Hermetica, was at the node just at the end of the block. They paused before going in. It was so low today, the sky, as though it began just at the top of the section walls. The walls didn't end, Dase knew, every block was itself like a sealed module, but the designers gave them something beautiful to look at overhead so they wouldn't have to stare at grey walls on all six sides. Dase would give anything to climb into that deep, rich blue. They sighed and walked through the double set of sliding doors.

Passing through Decontamination, Dase went straight to their office. Lingering in the common area would all but force the other therapists to ask them how their day was, and Dase couldn't bear the thought of that. "How's it going?" The cruelest question there was.

They sat down and let out the tears. When they could, they focused on breathing. Deep breaths. It wouldn't do to see a patient like this.

Every work assignment brings us closer. All of us or none of us. That's what they had been taught. Dase was supposed to feel proud of their work as a therapist, but it was impossible not to see the assignment as some kind of failing. They had been early selected for placement in a science cohort, and at the end of it all, Dase was barely a technician, while the others had gone on to great things. True, only one person in the cohort had been selected as a designer and, last they knew, sidetracked into an Entertainment project, as far from the sky as Dase themself. And it was also true that officially, all jobs were equally valued and prestige ranking was discouraged. Appreciative commentary on this or that work category was boosted or muted accordingly, and even palliative therapists and cleaning bot repair overseers got their digital love. But people could still distinguish what was pihessay—what was forced—and what was genuinely admirable.

It was even worse in a science cohort, because the peer-revieweds structurally could not use the same metrics as the social, and if your name never dropped in a piharvee, you were, definitively, nobody.

But it was not the lack of name recognition that chafed Dase. If they could help make the sky every single day, and in exchange they had to be classed as "permanent reconciliation" on their profile for all the cohort to see, if no one ever knew that they made those colors, those moonrises, those soul-hemorrhaging sunsets, they would be perfectly happy.

It was the fact that they spent three and a half days a week guiding point prods and air jets over the knotted backs and shoulders of those who did the real work, that they coached the creators of beautiful and important things on corrective posture, that stifled their spirit.

Once they were breathing normally, Dase called the console to life and clocked in. The first appointment came in, seating and undressing on the other side of the plexi. They were a young person in mechanics from the next block over who had started seeking therapy a few months ago for soreness and migraines. The two had talked on other occasions, when Dase was on the up. They had a decent job, working on power supply and reducing distribution loss between blocks. The unending quest to make *Hermetica* more efficient. It wasn't genius work, but anything that might accelerate the arrival window was considered at least a little prestigious. Honestly, anything that involved working on the ship and not just on the bodies that filled it or the secondary machines that serviced it was considered decent. Dase had never worked on anyone who worked on the sky. Or the engines for that matter. It would be illicit, but Dase wondered whether those job descriptions were tracked to higher grade therapists.

The scan was complete, and Dase began directing their array of instruments over the patient's back, keeping half an eye on the display that emarenned all the neural activity, but mostly just following their own feelings on what the other body needed, how it responded to the probing, the vibrations, the digipressure, the heat, and the cold of the dozen different appendages they kept in motion on the other side of the plexi.

Dase supposed they were pretty good at what they did. There had even been comments on social that spoke of "a magic touch" that didn't seem to be pihessay, they were pretty sure they had been written by real patients and weren't just machine love to cheer them up. For all its prosaic lack of glamor, therapy was something Dase could do when they were down and when they were up. They could feel what other people were feeling, in a way it had surprised Dase to learn most other people could not.

And that was the world Dase inhabited. A jungle of raw feelings in which they were, at the same time, cold and alone.

On a prior appointment, Dase had asked this patient if they knew anything about the arrival window, but the mechanic wasn't that high up. And there wasn't really anything else they could ask someone like that, certainly nothing that had any bearing on their block. The power worked, except when it didn't, but it always came back quickly, and emergency systems never failed. Every now and then, a pihessay went out and they were all asked to minimize usage between such and such hours. Surely there was a lot of work involved behind the scenes, but, what to say? So, Dase conducted the session in silence.

The thought of the arrival window stayed with them, though. The arrival window was always narrowing and widening based on the complex interaction between the colleagues in Phys and the ones in Engineering, an interaction Dase was not privy to and would not understand anyway. But as it stood most recently, *Hermetica* was scheduled to arrive in two to three hundred years. At best, unless Bioeng, CogPhys, and Metaphys made some huge advancements, Dase would live just past the halfway point. They would never arrive. They would spend their life correcting the knots and cramps of engineers and designers who would put those knots right back in place with their next week of desk work. Even the ones who had completely aitcheff interfaces, no typing, all verbal and gestural commands, had posture problems. After all, many of the high tier specialists voluntarily worked seven days a week, "to keep their edge sharp," as the old saying went. So it was probably an enbihess: a problem that would Never Be Solved. Which meant that Dase's entire purpose was to keep fixing those reappearing knots. Forever and ever unto death. And that was all there would be.

After two more appointments, Dase went home for the day. And that's when Snookums appeared. Crossing the block, almost back to the module, they saw movement out of the corner of their eye. Dase turned, and there was a cat.

None of their neighbors had cats like that. Well, Dase couldn't actually be sure. Weeks passed before any one person had the chance to spend time with even half the people on their block. But getting assigned a new cat: that was something people bullhorned on social, every time. Vids, anecdotes, and a flurry of commentary. Dase would have noticed a cat like this.

Ash and coal in tiger stripes with peach cream undertones, the cat had a peremptory gaze set over a broad, majestic nose that came to the perfect little *fleur-de-lis* pawprint of a tip, a sculpted kiblet of marzipan perched over a pursed mouth flanked by long fans of whiskers that bespoke a scornful elegance.

The mystery cat ran up to the nearest wall, shoring up its confidence perhaps, but also inciting attention.

"Hey, Snookums," Dase said on a whim. Not knowing why, they lowered their mask. Not strictly permitted, out in the street, but no neighbors happened to be traversing the block at this hour. "Hey baby."

Dase made kissing sounds and Snookums, as it were, came hither. The feel of its fur was so warm and soft, some kind of liquid pleasure flowed through Dase's body and they drank it up, parched, like one coming in from the desert. They immediately felt their trapezius relax, releasing weeks of built up tension they should have noticed; it was after all in the center of their limited field of expertise. But while a patient begged a diagnosis, the self always demurred.

Having rubbed thoroughly against Dase's leg, Snookums ran suggestively ahead, right up to the door of the module. Dase's module.

"I don't suppose it's any harm if I borrow you for a bit."

As they approached, the module door slid open, and Snookums waltzed right inside as though it owned the place.

"Well," they joked. "They can't say I kidnapped you."

The bed extracted and Dase plopped down on top of it. Snookums jumped up and soon was atop their lower back, purring and kneading away. Even more tension dissolved, as though chains had been wrapped around Dase's lungs, and they re-encountered the tears forced down that morning, and so many other mornings. Now there were no more walls, and no need to man them, and Dase surrendered every last tear to the bed sheets. By the time Snookums jumped off, Dase felt dry and clean. Lighter.

They let the cat hang around until well after the beginning of the night cycle, stroking its head and flattering it with a progression of increasingly ridiculous superlatives, and then let it out the door. Snookums disappeared into the dark. Later they scrolled through all their neighbor's socials. None of them had a new cat.

———

Dase woke up with the certainty it was a special day. As soon as their feet hit the floor, the bed retracted and the smell of coffee infused the air.

"Good morning!" they chirped.

"Good morning, Dase."

The blinds rolled up with a satisfying rustle, like a whisper in reverse, and Dase saw that the designers had outdone themselves again. Another beautiful day aboard *Hermetica!*

By the time they fell to a crouch, the floor panel had transed to sturdy foam, and Dase launched themself into a dozen short reps of crunches, squats, and burpees. As they came down from the final leap, fingers almost touching the module's roof, they were panting joyfully.

They did a few stretches while their breathing came down, heel up on the window sill. The shower extracted the moment they pulled their underpants down, right on cue. The jets were hot and precise and Dase found bliss in the barrage of water. They didn't exactly have time to think before the liter ran out, but to feel, certainly. They felt a wonderful day stretch out before them.

They toweled off and tossed it, along with yesterday's clothes, into the chute, which closed and vacked them away. The shower dehumidified with a gentle roar as Dase selected a new set of clothes, a loose baggy shirt, and some snug elastic pants that would offer no objections, they thought capriciously, if later they felt like dancing.

As soon as they took a seat, the emmery chuted out onto the table, piping hot, its farther edge making a perfect tangent with the coffee mug at its side. Just the way they liked it.

"Would you like a dose, this morning?"

"No thanks! I'm ready to meet the world on my own, today!"

Module had already predicted that response based on Dase's vitals and visuals. But it also knew that being asked and saying no, affirming their ability to go without chemical supplementation, increased the average time before Dase would again need a dose.

Breakfast was pretty good, a palette of flavors with names like bacon, mango, and plantain cast across a satisfying diversity of textures. As they finished up the last bites, they decided, hell, they could go all out.

"Calendar?"

"Yes, Dase."

"Who's my social appointment for today?"

"Milty."

"Oh, good! Send a confirmation. Also a message."

"Recording."

"Hey Milty! I'm looking forward to seeing you today! Do you feel like coming over? I hope so. I'm cooking! Don't bring anything. See you at... 19 aitch? Bye!"

"Sending."

"Thanks!"

"Shall I set your default to pre-confirmation on social appointments?"

"Wo-ho, Module! Let's not get ahead of ourselves," Dase chuckled. "Wait and see how we're feeling tomorrow, yeah?"

"Of course, Dase."

They stood up, pushing the empty emmery and mug into their chute.

"Oh Dase? Milty has confirmed for 19 aitch."

Great. It had been about a week since Dase had kept a social appointment. You only got one a day, plus the multi on Sundays, and the block party four times a year for everyone in good health. It had been like that ever since the New Safety was implemented, back when Dase was an infant. It turned out that the population on *Hermetica*, ideal for rapidly settling a new home world, was also the perfect ecosystem for the evolution and incubation of new viruses, and twenty-five years ago, an epidemic had raced through the close quarters of the ship. ARPV, popularly known as the choking sickness, had infected millions. It was only deadly in extreme cases, but it spread asymptomatically, making it exceedingly hard to control. The engineers and medicals had perfected the module and block layout, restricting transit across the entire system. Every cohort and every block was composed of people of the same age, preventing cross-generational contagion and protecting the more vulnerable age groups, while streamlining health services. And since then there had been no serious emergencies. They had adapted, what had been vigilance became custom, and life went on.

Mask on and out the door, Dase looked around for Snookums, but saw no sign of the cat. A number of their neighbors were out and about, and they sang out one good morning after another. The sky was projecting puffy white clouds and a strident sun, and Dase relished in the wind whipping about their face. The membrane that closed off the top of every block was permeable to air and precipitation, as *Hermetica*'s life support system needed to cycle oxygen, nitrogen, and water vapor on a ship-wide basis. The system was far from perfect, and occasionally there were simulated weather events to equalize pressure and chemical distribution. Fortunately, the designers could always anticipate weather occurrences with the data they got from Meteo, and they made sure the sky was always dressed for the occasion. So today, the clouds moved from left to right, in the same direction as the wind.

Coming to the center of the block, Dase saw they were building something on the Green. As a couple drones hovered about, movers deposited bundles and a couple bots erected a tall pole, almost as high as the tallest modules, the family units. Was it already time for the next block party? Dase wondered what the theme this time would be. The last one was Chinese New Year, but Dase hadn't been feeling well and gave it a miss.

Staying out of the way of the bots, they crossed the Green. The health center was straight ahead, but the supply node was to the right, at the end of the cross street. They had to get ingredients if they were going to cook for Milty tonight. But then they might be late for the first patient, and certainly too excited thinking about dinner to focus on work. They could stop by on the way home.

It was a fortuitous decision. First in the queue, they got a new patient. One who worked in Meteo. Bubbling with curiosity, they bit their tongue until the patient was comfortable and the ensemble of machines were whizzing and whirring over their back. It would not do to stress them out, compound whatever muscle problem had brought them here, and get a low rating on top of it all. Some people loved to talk during the sessions, but others flat out fell asleep.

"So you're a meteorologist?" Dase ventured after the patient let out a particularly appreciative groan.

"Me? No..."

Dase frowned.

"Nope, I work in Meteorology, but I'm actually a botanist."

Oh, good! A talker. "I thought all the botanists were in Alimentation?"

"Most of us, but not me. You know the bushes and shrubs that grow on your block?"

"Uh huh."

"Well, every block has a botanical cohort, you see, to complement the human population. Spread across *Hermetica*, we actually have quite a biodiversity in plant species. Of course, everything we'll need to terraform is in the Gene Bank, but there's a hypothesis that after a certain stage of chemprep, we'll have better luck transplanting adult specimens. In any case, with live stock, we have redundancy, and it's also proven to improve air quality and mental health for the passengers."

"Wow. Well, that makes sense. So... what's the connection with Meteorology?"

"Meteo's primary job is to monitor the atmosphere aboard *Hermetica*. Of course, the atmosphere belongs to Life Systems, their prime directive is to give us air to breathe. But any changes they make have ship-wide ramifications, so they have to work closely with Meteo to roll out those changes and monitor any feedback. Think of Meteo as like a shock absorber for LifeSys."

"Ah. And Botany?"

"Well we're the shock absorbers for the shock absorbers! A meteorology roll out is designed for the health of the passengers, while minimizing the kind of discomfort system ripples can cause. No one's thinking about the shrubs! So that's where I come in. Weather events and atmosphere in general spell life or death for our botany cohorts, and they're not very high up the priority chain. Now your maintenance bots are collecting chemical data every time they go by, and the block analyzes it, and sometimes can make a change autonomously. *Schizophragma* needs more watering? Done. But I combine that with qualitative commentary on plant health, I can override the block and design a special treatment regime for an unhealthy specimen, and in the case of prolonged malaise, I can make a recommendation to Meteo."

"Like, to change the weather?"

"You bet. If it can keep a cohort from dying off. Of course, like I said, it's low on the priority chain. But sometimes they make adjustments."

"Wow, that's amazing. I've never met anyone who can affect the weather before. So you're in charge of all the plants on *Hermetica*?"

The patient laughed. "Me? Naw. I just supervise a hundred blocks. No complaints here, that lets me travel way more than your average passenger. But *Hermetica*'s huge, and we each got our tiny role to play. If any one person just focuses on themself, they feel small, but what we're doing all together? It's extraordinary."

A shadow crossed over Dase's heart, the first of the day. The patient was right, it was extraordinary. But Dase couldn't help but feel like their life was impossibly small. Was it fair that one person could travel across a hundred blocks, could reach up and touch the sky—*could make it rain*—and Dase had to spend their life between the module and the office, not even a hundred meters apart, touching strangers through a plexi and the intermediary of a dozen probes and appendages?

It was their own fault, of course. If they had studied harder, they could have done better on the aptitudes. They had had all the advantages of an education in sciences. The other people from their cohort had gone on to important assignments. They didn't keep up with most of them, but they could see what they were doing on social. One, a mathematician, had created a dynamic encryption system that enabled classified reports to *read one another*, so that specialists from different working groups and with different security clearances could access relevant information across departments, or check their data directly against another set of data without having to actually view it, in the event they did not have clearance. Another, a molecular biologist, was working on a team perfecting a nanobotic array that could quickly scan, detect, analyze, and repair genetic mutations across an entire organism. Plenty had gone into Phys, and though physics people generally could not speak about their work, it was rumored that one of them was in the nuclear program, working on *Hermetica*'s propulsion system.

Zimp, Dase's best friend from the cohort, was in HigherEd, training the next generation of minds in quantum mechanics. Axa, another classmate, was in Sociopsych, designing optimum human interactions. Definitely not Dase's cup of tea, but who was Dase to be picky? They were a masseuse, running the same dozen routines over variants of the same four problems, over and over and over again. The training, post-aptitudes, was simple: a year of anatomy and then a month of technical education for operating the machines. Dase had figured it out in a week. Zimp, on the other hand, had gone through six years of training, and had to do hours of reading every week to keep up on the piharvees. And the molecular biologist from the cohort had only gotten a work assignment a couple years ago, after eight years of post-ap training.

If Dase had been feeling a little better, more social, the day of the aptitudes, would the outcome have been any different? They had scored well in analytical and maths, but the low teamwork score had spelled doom for just about any cutting edge assignment.

Dreading the memory, they were back in the unfamiliar room. Most of the faces were unfamiliar too. Cohorts got broken up for testing. The young students in the room were joined by another bond, though. Who could fail to recognize the shared anxiety, to know oneself in one's peers? The examiner was late. No one was happy about that. The screen at the front of the class already read 9:20. That was starting time. They were supposed to have two and a half full hours to finish.

Dase looked around, weighing their peer's growing concern. The ubiquitous "Remember the *Wiki*" poster hung, forlorn, on the back wall. There were no windows.

At 9:24:36, the door swished open and the examiner bustled in, taking their place at the head console. Their face was austere, not a sign of fluster or apology. Everyone in the class shifted, backs erect, hands at the ready atop their desks.

The examiner logged in and entered a command, and the console extracted from everyone's desk. Twenty sets of fingers launched themselves atop tactile screens, entering personal id numbers and pass codes. Any moment, the first problem should appear.

Instead, the examiner spoke. Speaking was strictly forbidden during the aptitudes, but they were the examiner. They could have you removed and failed for the mere suspicion of impropriety.

"Before the test begins, you will all go into config and set the test time back to 9:20:00. Use this override." A twelve digit pass code appeared on the main screen.

That was certainly irregular. And it hardly seemed fair. They had now lost five full minutes from their testing time, and no one ever got through all the problems. Dase decided not to comply. Still, frightened of the examiner, they moved their fingers over the tactile so they'd blend in with all the others.

Then the test started, and the first problem appeared on everyone's screen.

Dase was delighted to find Snookums waiting at the module door when they walked up, arms full of groceries from the supply node. Module opened to let the two of them in, and Dase gave the cat a good scratch behind the ear as soon as the groceries were safely atop the table. They had gotten more than enough ingredients for dinner. Real tomatoes, basil, garlic, onion, mushrooms, ricotta, mozzarella, red paste, petribeef, eggsub, fresh lasagna noodles: they'd had a backlog of credit, having canceled the last week of socials. If they weren't feeling up for a social, they usually weren't feeling up for cooking, and emmeries were unlimited, just a voice command away.

Dase was reputed to be the best cook on the block. There was not much competition, but still, it was nice to be valued for something. As long as they canceled social appointments on bad days, friendship with Dase was a cherished commodity. The meals they whipped up balanced out their unpredictability, the fact that so often, they simply did not show up. In truth, it worked out quite well. They needed at least five day's worth of credit to get enough fresh ingredients for a good meal. Taking on too many socials just wouldn't be tenable.

"Axa just released a new list, shall I put it on?"

Of course, Module knew that Dase nearly always listened to music while cooking, and Axa's lists were highly rated, but today Dase had a specific melody worming its way through their brain.

"No. Put on Dvořak, Slavonic Dance 1. Um, the 46."

The orchestra erupted pleasantly through the module's walls, and Dase started on the prep, chopping the onion, mincing half the garlic. "Front left burner, medium high. Front right burner, medium." They placed two pans on the range, dripped in some olive oil. Next they converted the mushroom into thin slices. There was an autocutter built into the wall next to the range, but Dase relished the contact, the differing textures and resistance of the vegetables, the weight and inexorable finality of the knife, a simple machine that abetted rather than forestalled entropy. The pans were already hot, they put the onions in one, the garlic in the other. The violins and flutes pranced with a deceptive gaiety before the bassoons came in and then the whole thing rocketed to its frenetic finale.

The applause thundered. Who were those people clapping? It must be a recorded concert from back on Terra. *Hermetica* was big, but Dase had never heard of it having a concert hall or a full symphony orchestra. Module cycled on to Slavonic Dance 7, following Dase's biostats, their reaction to the previous piece, current activity.

Dase had tried learning an instrument once, but had little talent, or perhaps a lack of consistency. They were fascinated by music, though. One of the quirks of enteekay and the New Safety was that people tracked for the sciences had little access to studies on history, culture, and philosophy, basically any of the extraneous product of Terran civilization. Perhaps the architects of *Hermetica* had wanted a clean break. The Terrans had discovered thermodynamics, very well, but why weigh themselves down with all the other baggage of a self-destructive society? So they had libraries full of dismembered artifacts—from novels to waltzes—but little about the stories behind them.

Dase often found themself wondering about the people who had created such beautiful music. They had first gotten hooked while studying for the aptitudes, when certain kinds of music were boosted for improving focus and retention. Really, they were only familiar with thirty odd pieces by a half dozen composers, didn't understand the weird number/word system for cataloguing symphonies, nor what dramatic experiences the composers were drawing on, yet something undeniable was there, reaching across the void to commune.

Dase turned back to the task at hand. As the melody twirled and slowed, joyous and grave, a whirlwind of life on the precipice of despair, they scooped the petribeef in with the garlic and shook on a generous dusting of cayenne. It was going to be a beautiful supper.

Dase stole a moment on the couch with Snookums, running their thumb between the cat's shoulder blades as it purred blissfully. Before long, though, they had to get back to the range, stirring the beef, the onions, adding the mushrooms to the onions, salting them. Module picked the next score, Shostakovich's Second Waltz.

"Preheat oven to 190. Front right burner to high. Front left off."

They whipped together the ricotta and the eggsub, opened the red paste, oiled the oven pan, and topped a layer of red paste with the first layer of lasagna. The petribeef was sizzling, they turned off the last burner, and then continued layering, veggies meat and red paste, lasagna, ricotta, lasagna. Mozzarella on top when all the layers were in place. Then into the oven.

Dase could make the salad later, the tomatoes would be best if served freshly chopped. They hurried back to the couch, where Snookums was still kneading the fabric and staring at them seductively. Horns sounded, quietly at first, then joined by trombones, strings, woodwinds. They had forgotten about the music. Module had cycled on to the 11th Symphony.

Milty should be arriving in an hour. Perfect timing. Snookums shifted its weight against Dase's thigh, and the two of them blissed out, carried along by the symphony's rising emotion, now tragic, now heroic.

Suddenly it was time to take the lasagna out, slice the tomatoes, mince the basil and garlic, and then Milty was there.

Milty had gone into organic chemistry, and their work had something to do with growing tissue samples or replacement organs that Dase did not fully understand. Most of the time, they worked from home, going over lab results or conducting tests by remote, but every now and then they got to go into campus, some twenty blocks away. The standard block had four nodes, one on each end of the two perpendicular streets. A health center, a supply node, a maintenance center, and some other work station, different for every block. Those who did not work at either of those four stations worked from home as much as possible—vectors on *Hermetica* had to be kept to a constant minimum—but scientific research was a major priority on board. *Hermetica* had set out from Terra with a solid design and a trajectory towards a cluster of star systems with a high number of promising exoplanets, but the greater part of their mission resources were *in potentia*, the cohorts of advanced scientists who were constantly improving the ship's propulsion, making sure life systems could function for five hundred years with no external inputs, and augmenting their terraforming kits to be ready for whatever the conditions were on the exoplanet they eventually settled. None of that had ever been done before.

Laboratories were the largest spaces on the ship, entire blocks, or several adjacent blocks, fitted out as scientific campuses. Dase had no idea how many there were in total, but Milty was lucky enough to work at one of them. And they were kind enough to only tell stories that helped Dase appreciate how large their world was, without feeling envious about being confined to such a small part of it. Dase liked Milty.

After dinner, they put on a movie. A new one that paired Humphrey Bogart and Robin Williams in an old-style Western, the first two in a probe team to land on Mars. Dase loved listening to Milty laugh.

The film was Milty's recommendation. Dase had rarely enjoyed Westerns in the past, but they could not think of any other new release to recommend. In the end they had to admit, Bogart played the perfect straight—hard-jawed, eyes on the mission—as Williams went crazy, itching at the regolith that got inside their suit or getting in a shouting match with the air miner.

"Bravo," Dase said when it was over.

"You liked it? Oh, I'm glad."

"I needed to laugh today."

"So I have a question," Milty said. They knew Dase loved to discuss films as soon as they were done, and they always indulged them. A film studies elective had been one of Dase's favorite courses in school, covering everything from sound engineering to narrative technique, an introduction for those who would go on to work in Entertainment. The teacher, a kindly, bearded old person, often diverged into the long history of the craft, pre-exploration, and those tangential lectures, refracted through the lens of dolly zooms and fourth walls, were the source of much of what Dase knew about Terra.

"Ask away."

"Why do they call them Westerns? I thought "west" was a Terran positional reference. It can only map onto a planetary surface, relative to rotation, right? So is it a cultural thing? I remember some Terrans referred to themselves as Western." There was in fact an esoteric joke about primitives on Terra only moving in one direction, counter to the planet's rotational spin.

Dase knew the answer to this one. It was true that the protagonists of Westerns were always pasty-skinned, and the bad guys—if there were any, besides misbehaving air miners and silicate factories—had their skin darkened, or in neo-Westerns, painted green. As a child, Dase had assumed it was in fact the protagonists who painted their skin in some bizarre Old World status aesthetic. After all, nearly all the people they had seen with such pasty skin were Terran actors. The film teacher, though, had explained that in Old World Terra, before the explorations began, the pasty-skinned phenotype had dominated the film industry and only cast themselves in the leading roles. What a bizarre place Terra must have been. And what a relief that *Hermetica* and all its passengers had left Terra far behind them.

"Actually, there are pretty specific generic requirements. A Western is a retrospective science fiction set in what was considered to be a primitive or low-tech frontier."

"Wow. You really paid attention in class."

"Are you kidding? I ate that shit up. All electives, not enough focus on the core material," they said with a wry grin. "A sure track to being a palliative therapist or a cleaner."

"Hey, Dase. I would rather watch movies with you than with any of my work colleagues. So don't stop, lay more of this knowledge on me. Retrospective science fiction?"

"Yeah. The story is set in a place in the past, so low technology relative to the audience, and in a territory they'll identify as especially primitive and chaotic. Yet at the same time, it's a territory that has been tamed and organized by the time the people are there watching the movie, a space that in fact might then be identified as being at the cutting edge of their technological development. So you have Humphrey Bogart bumbling around on Mars in Terra's first attempt at extraterrestrial inhabitation, John Wayne playing "suck the cesium" on the Nevada Test Site... I guess the first works in the genre would be *The Tempest* or *The Aeneid*."

By this point, Dase was just riffing. Their old teacher had mentioned the fact about John Wayne's demise, satisfaction and bitterness waging some unexplained battle across their face, but the literary references were connections Dase had come up with in the moment, no way to evaluate their historical validity, certainly no studies to cite; simply a pattern that suddenly felt right, obvious even.

"So why Western?"

"Oh, I guess it's a coincidence, but most of the Classical or Modern Westerns involved geographical travel to the west on the planetary surface. Not the case with neo-Westerns, but by that time the name had already stuck."

Feeling fully comfortable now, or desirous of more attention, Snookums got in Dase's lap. Milty hadn't mentioned it yet, which was odd: Snookums had been rubbing against Dase's legs or purring on the couch between the two for the whole movie.

"So this cat just appeared yesterday."

"What cat?" Milty asked earnestly, still smiling.

Snookums flicked its tail in sudden displeasure.

"Oh. Never... long story."

"No, tell me," Milty smiled again in encouragement.

"I was..." Dase knew not to push it. People saw what they were going to see. And most of them hated the idea that not everyone saw the same thing. "I was thinking of applying for a companion animal."

"Oh, that's great!"

"I saw one yesterday. The profile, I mean. Looks really cute."

Snookums jumped off Dase's lap in a huff. Milty still didn't notice.

"I'm sure you'll get approved. There's not too many on our block, you have a good record, you work in therapy." They didn't add that mental health index was also a factor. Didn't need to. "I bet you'll get your first choice, too. What's it look like? The cute one?"

Snookums began scratching the side of the couch in patent irritation.

"Like a troublemaker. Hey, do you want dessert?" Dase had to change the subject fast, before Milty asked to see the profile.

Milty went home after dessert. Snookums was still huffy, scratching at a wall panel as Dase put the dishes in the chute. Their mood was starting to crash. Why did socials always end up making them feel more alone?

"Hey Module, put the music back on?" Accusatory notes rang out sharply, Shostakovich's Symphony No. 13 according to the screen. Snookums began scratching more furiously, as though it wanted to be heard over the strings.

"Hey, I'm sorry. Some people just don't want to see. What was I supposed to do?" Dase walked over and picked the cat up, hugging it tightly. Snookums forbore, then resisted, and finally Dase let it spring to the floor.

"Hey, you did some damage here." Dase knelt down. The corner of the wall panel had actually come loose. That wasn't good. But instead of pushing it back into place—the module was largely self-repairing, and a little nudge to realign the panel might solve the whole thing—Dase began pulling. They had never seen what was behind a wall panel, and at the moment, the perfect stability of their environment felt like mockery. It was a feeling which Dase would be unable to explain, yet at the same time was absolutely certain: the walls exuded scorn, they condescended, they knew things they assumed Dase was unable to see, and they belittled their attempts to think freely.

"Continuing may cause structural damage."

"It's okay, Module, I'm trying to fix it. Actually, I need you to release this panel so I can put it back in properly, it's misaligned."

Most systems were self-regulating, and Module's data certainly indicated that Dase was, in fact, wrong. But a standard AI parameter allowed human intervention to override system decisions in cases where the risk only encompassed a single element and not the whole system. Human perception, however imprecise, was open-ended, and system criteria had to come from passengers anyway, so Module relented. The wall panel came free.

It was not the destructive release Dase had been hoping for, nothing like taking a hammer to the whole structure. But on *Hermetica*, all forms of release were modulated through the paramount need to compromise.

The gesture's inevitable disappointment, however, evaporated immediately. Mystery took its place, for the moment the panel came free, a sheet that had been tucked behind it fell to the ground. Snookums took a seat beside it, looking up at Dase pointedly.

"Um." Dase's hands began to tremble. Remembering their alibi, they quickly stuck the panel back in the wall. "Okay, that should do it."

"Panel is aligned and secured."

Their mouth dry, Dase picked the sheet up off the floor. Its texture was strange, brittle, its tones muted and dirty. It was covered with minuscule writing on both sides, but when Dase tried to enlarge, nothing happened. Had it been back there so long, it had run out of battery? They shook it a few times and tried again. Nothing. A device like that should be piezoelectric, but maybe it was malfunctioned, maybe that was why it had been discarded back there. Dase stood and brought the sheet to the range. If it had any internal circuits, even malfunctioning ones, the range would detect them, recharge them, and if possible, repair them. Nothing. The range did not recognize the sheet as electronic.

Dase looked closer, twisted an edge of it. It seemed to be made of some kind of fiber, and not one they were familiar with.

Well, they'd have to do this the old-fashioned way. Squinting, they began to read.

Along the top, there was a date. June 12, 2023. Below a yellowing margin, an article began.

Experts: As Vaccine Hopes Falter, Choking Sickness Here To Stay

Health officials warn that America may have to get used to semi-permanent confinement measures, as results from the latest vaccine trial at the University of Washington failed to deliver good news to a nation that is still grieving the catastrophic mismanagement during the first two years of the ARPV-20 pandemic. Recent studies confirm early fears that the virus may mutate too quickly to allow for long-term immunity.

Officials underscored that confinement is a positive measure compared with the inferno the virus left in its wake during the period of governmental inaction. "We will not go back to the horrors of the Party system, putting the comfort of the few before the survival of the many," said Dr. Goa, speaking from the steps of the National Health Administration. "We are currently expanding the parameters of our modeling, looking for innovative solutions to this crisis. Believe us when we say, increasing human life expectancy across the board, for all Americans, is our number one metric. If we have to delete elements from the old system in order to fulfill that promise, we will do so. We ask all Americans to walk with us, boldly, into the future we are building. We will respect tradition, but we must cast aside the harmful habits that hold us back."

Officials are worried about a resurgence of last year's unrest amid an uptick in terrorist incidents. All incidents linked to loss of life have been connected to market extremists and traditionalists who, even after a million deaths, still deny the pandemic exists. More worrying for the Administration, however, is the increase in sabotage incidents carried out by social extremists. Relative to the denialists, social extremists have more influence among the general population, and experts worry they could lead people astray with unrealistic demands or magical solutions.

Speaking from the White House, Dr. Hennessy, chair of the Planning Commission, warned that social extremist proposals were "nothing but vestigial, anti-scientific superstition. They claim to speak for quality of life, but by adding archaic, non-quantitative metrics alongside quantitative metrics, they wreck the whole system. It doesn't compute. Tell me, what is fifteen times orange? This is intellectual anarchy. It's idealistic. It doesn't work. They need to get with the program. It's the 21st century. If you can't model it, don't propose it."

Increasing quality of life metrics before the Trial Period ends will be necessary for the Administration to carry the referendum early next year. Otherwise, the state of emergency will expire and the old Constitution, which most experts agree is unworkable, would come back into effect.

Meanwhile, the growing pool of pandemic orphans has required officials to increase social spending beyond what was earmarked for the fiscal year. Social officials promise to look into innovative solutions. Speaking from the NSA's offices in Omaha, Dr. Ventura gave journalists a hint of a new project the Social Administration was exploring.

"At the NSA, we believe all life has value. Under the old system, orphans were just warehoused in substandard facilities until a family with means could come along and adopt them. Need and capacity were inversely proportional. In a recession, more kids get abandoned, and fewer families can adopt them. We are rolling out a new system in which the parentless are given everything they need, including a top-of-the-line education, and in the meantime we'll track their performance, collect data, and produce intellectual value that will be immediately useful for the rest of society. Everyone wants to contribute. We'll give these kids the opportunity to contribute from day one, from the cradle."

Ventura's comments provided a rare optimistic note at a time when the scientific solutions promised by the Planning Commission seem unlikely to bear fruit. Given the poor results of the vaccine program, Commission aides, speaking on condition of anonymity, say that plans for defunding the police will be delayed again, given expectations of a spike in civil unrest. *cont'd on page 12*

Dase flipped over the sheet, but "page 12," whatever that was, was nowhere to be found. The back side had a large illustration of some kind of wheeled vehicle, and the beginning of another article.

Planet Earth Our Only Hope?
Mars Probe Results Lead to Pessimistic Conclusions

In a much delayed report, NASA conceded that permanent human habitation on Mars seemed unlikely, given the results from the last probes sent to the Red Planet. Obstacles include the toxicity of the Martian regolith, with its high concentrations of perchlorates, difficulties in filtering out the ultra-fine Martian dust particles, also toxic, and strong limitations on the availability of energy sources and organic chemicals needed for terraforming.

The report is grave news for sectors of the scientific community that have proposed accelerated terraforming on Mars as an answer to the cascading chain of catastrophes adversely affecting Earth's own biosphere.

"We will just have to accelerate the terraforming of Earth, as it were," said Dr. Stewart, chairperson of the Climate Advisory Council. "That means aggressive reengineering of the biosphere to design agricultural ecosystems compatible with 5° warming, rather than waiting for 1-2 million years of evolutionary adaptation to play catch-up."

The report may also be a death knell for the space agency itself, one of the few to be kept on from the prior government. Perhaps realizing the report would spell trouble, NASA's leading scientists have been lobbying the Planning Commission to change the agency's mandate to a focus on orbital space engineering with an eye towards climate mitigation. One of the agency's most popular proposals centers on the deployment of orbital mirrors to fine tune the quantity of solar radiation that reaches the planet's surface. *cont'd on page 17*

Dase was thoroughly confused. Shostakovich declaimed ominously, like a fist on the door. Snookums sat, watching.

The dating and the geographical references were all Terran. "Earth" was an archaic name for Terra. Yet the choking sickness had been an event on *Hermetica*. Where was this sheet from? What was it doing here? The events described were a muddle, some of them lining up with what they knew of Terran history, and others contradicting it flagrantly.

Dase decided to reach out to a friend. "Message Zimp. Hey, are you still up? Do you remember from history, what year did *Hermetica* launch?"

The reply came back a moment later, announced by an amiable rising tone. "Dase, how's it going? What a question."

Zimp had been assigned to a different block after the aptitudes, but they still saw each other on video every now and then.

The recording continued. "You know, you could just ask Library. But that's an easy one. Technically, it's a trick question, *Hermetica* never launched, it was assembled in orbit, but it departed in Terran year 2022. Seven years later, we left the solar system."

"And what year is it now? On Terra."

Zimp replied. "I guess it must be 2050. Why do you ask?"

"Oh, just trying to work some things out. Hey, do you think we could do a video call? Like, soon?"

"Sure."

"Good night, Zimp."

"Good night, Dase. Talk soon."

The bed extracted with fresh sheets and Dase plopped down, cradling Snookums against their chest. Sleep came fitful and late.

The next day, Dase messaged that they wouldn't be going in to work. They tried sleeping longer, but it was impossible. Their brain wouldn't quit. After half an hour of tossing and turning, they found themself locked in the reenactment of a fierce argument with the examiner, the day of the aptitudes. It was all imagination. They had never actually confronted the examiner, or anyone else. But since the day the results came back, thwarting their dreams, whittling their future down to nothing, they had spent many hours inside their head, protesting the unfairness of it all. Who was to say that the examiner's tardiness had not disadvantaged them relative to other testing groups?

As far as Dase's low teamwork scores, surely there was more than one way to measure teamwork. On the aptitudes, at three different moments, people's screens were linked in groups of five, and each group had to solve a common problem, communicating over their devices but not speaking directly. Dase had not integrated effectively into the problem solving, but building an effective team could play out differently if people were allowed to talk directly, make eye contact, if they didn't have a ticking clock hanging over their heads.

Other aspects of the aptitudes were borderline shoddy. Dase could only remember one error, aside from the examiner arriving late. But still, an error on such an important test did not give a good impression. In a problem on emissions spectra, video of an experiment appeared on Dase's screen, showing an unidentified compound burning bright green. Before anyone had gotten to that problem, the examiner had made another verbal announcement: "On problem 41, there was an error in experiment preparation. Substitute the flame color you see on your personal console with the flame color pictured here." They gestured, and a video of a dark red flame appeared on the main screen.

But the exams were computer evaluated. How could Dase be sure the examiner was not the one who was mistaken? Puzzled, annoyed, they had skipped the question and gone on to the next one. How could it possibly be considered fair for their future to be determined on the basis of such an errant instrument?

In their head, they always won those arguments, but when it was over they still had to face up to the same reality.

Annoyed, they got out of bed, called for a coffee, reluctantly declined the dose Module offered, and then squared off against the wall screen.

"Take me to the library."

The wall screen came on.

"Show me Hermetica."

A grainy schematic appeared, showing the image Dase knew well from school. *Hermetica* was an immensely long, slender cylinder with a rounded nose and a bulky tail where the propulsion reactors were housed. Arrayed sequentially along its length were four rings, each connected to the central cylinder by gossamer spokes. Given the dimensions of the ship, Dase knew each spoke must be incredibly thick, but in the schematic, they always looked so delicate. The rings were modified Stanford toruses. Rather than being a continuous loop like a donut, as in the standard torus, each ring held three immense platforms, evenly spaced about the circumference. It was like a torus, but with three parts of the loop symmetrically blotted out. In profile they looked like circular arcs with θ of 30°. The rings rotated slowly, and all the blocks, every module, every person Dase had ever known, were housed on the inside of one of the twelve platforms, held in place by the pseudogravity created by centrifugal force.

If it weren't for the sky, they would be able to look up and see *Hermetica*'s central cylinder about ten kilometers above them, bisecting their view, and on either side of it, even farther away, the other two platforms on their ring. Actually, Dase supposed, they would only see any of that if they turned off all the lights on their platform, and if the material closing off the top of the platform, from their frame of reference, the inside of the arc, were transparent. Otherwise, above them they would see a massive reflection or glare. In any case, before *Hermetica* had even departed, its builders knew that mental health stats improved greatly if a sky were projected diffusing light and replicating the heavens people had evolved under, on Terra.

Dase tried to remember which of the twelve platforms they lived on. Had that been taught in school?

"Zoom in."

The perspective shifted vertiginously, diving in close, and suddenly Dase was looking at their block and the eight blocks that flanked it, four of them sharing a node with theirs. It was not much wider of a view than the one they were stuck in every day.

"Library, can I get a... a more intermediate view? Ship schematics?"

"Since the destruction of the *Wiki*, access to precise schematics for *Hermetica* are compartmentalized on a Need To Know basis."

Yeah, the *Wiki* disaster and the infamous enteekay. Dase had heard all about that. They sighed. "Well... can you show me where we're going?"

Library switched to a live feed from a camera. Part of the screen revealed the observation window at the tip of *Hermetica*'s nose. Most of it was the blackness of space, dotted with a million pinpricks. Three of the pinpricks directly in front of them were noticeably larger, one of them twice as bright as anything else on the screen. Still, though, just a pinprick. And Dase would never get there, never see its planets up close.

"Can we get a view of Terra?"

"The solar system is not currently visible from the cameras on the rear ring. Would you like the rear view anyway?"

Dase sighed again. "No, that's alright." Another thought occurred to them. "Bring up Terran history, the decades prior to departure."

A list of topic headers appeared on the screen.

"What do you have on epidemics?"

A long list scrolled by, listing names, dates, locations, death tolls. Dase saw some they remembered from basic history, others that were unfamiliar. Dengue fever, Ebola, cholera, swine flu, yellow fever, AIDS, Spanish influenza, typhus.

"What about choking sickness?"

Library paused. "Choking sickness was not a Terran event. Choking sickness, ARPV, was an event here on *Hermetica*. Would you like to see the entry?"

"No, that's alright, I'm looking for Terran epidemics. Was there anything else that might have been similar? What does ARPV stand for?"

"Acute Respiratory Passenger Virus."

Passenger virus. Well, that certainly sounded like the name of a disease that would break out on a ship.

"What's the last year you have entries for, in Terran history?"

"2022."

Dase looked at the sheet in their hand. One year before the article was published. One year: there had been a reference to something that had happened a year earlier. There it was.

"Unrest. Tell me about political unrest from 2022. Umm, in America."

"Here is the disambiguation on America. Please specify."

"Oh. Scroll down? Yeah, that one. United States of America."

"There are no entries on significant political unrest in the United States of America in 2022."

"Hmmm. What about denialists."

"Here is the disambiguation on denialists. Please specify."

There weren't many choices, and the first one seemed to be a simple dictionary definition, *one who denies an empirically demonstrated fact*. "How about... climate denialists?"

"Climate denialists were political pressure groups funded by hydrocarbon extraction industries who claimed that the significant increase in heat-trapping gases in the planet's atmosphere would not trap heat in the planet's atmosphere. Hydrocarbon extraction industries in the United States began funding climate denialists sometime after 1968, when their research demonstrated conclusively that their product was in fact changing the chemical composition of Terra's atmosphere in a significant way."

That didn't sound like what the article was talking about. It sounded like bad fiction. But the reference had to do with a pandemic, not with the atmosphere.

Dase shook their head, not sure if they were amused or appalled by the concept of a global hydrocarbon energy system. They thought back to basic chemistry. Sure, it made sense to transport hydrocarbon fuel for use in remote locations not reached by an electrical grid, if none of the vehicles involved were large enough to house nuclear reactors. But systematically burning hydrocarbons in vehicles that traveled standard routes, each lugging the weight of its own combustion engines? Or to power the entire electrical grid burning the stuff? They had put tens of millions of years of sequestered carbon into the atmosphere in a century. What a relief *Hermetica* had left that place behind. Dase felt bad for the segment of humanity that stayed behind.

Still, the present conundrum had not become any clearer. Dase had come up against a wall. The information in the article and the information in the library did not add up. Then they remembered the second article, the one on the back of the sheet. From the talk of failed probes, they inferred that Mars had not been settled in Terran year 2023. But if Mars had not even been settled yet, how had they managed to send off *Hermetica* a full year earlier?

"Library, tell me about the human colonization of Mars."

"After the first unoccupied probes landed on the Martian surface in 1971 and 1975, work began on larger spacecraft that could transport human astronauts. By the time an assembly and launching platform had been manufactured in low Earth orbit in 1998, further probes to Mars had carried out all the mapping and chemical analysis necessary to begin planning the logistics of a human mission. Supply drops to the Martian surface began the next year, and the first occupied spacecraft was launched from the orbital platform in 2007, arriving safely with its twelve person crew ten months later. They remained for two Terran years, overseeing construction of the research station and launch platform, returning safely to Terra in 2011.

"By that point, it was clear that Mars' chemical and circumstellar characteristics were unfavorable to terraforming, and it was calculated that it would actually be cheaper and faster to terraform an exoplanet in the Goldilocks zone of another star system, even accounting for a journey of several hundred Terran years. Activity based out of the Mars research station continued, carried out remotely or by subsequent human teams."

Dase scratched their head. They supposed the probes mentioned in the article could have been from subsequent attempts to explore other avenues of terraforming on Mars, in parallel to preparations on the *Wiki* and *Hermetica* missions. Still, it didn't say anything about a research station or any human presence on Mars, nor did it mention the two ships that had departed the year before, with millions of passengers between them.

Something didn't add up. Dase looked crossly at the strange, printed sheet. All published material was vetted and peer-reviewed by pertinent experts. Affirmations of fact were always qualified, results that had not been rigorously replicated included margins of error or the probabilities of some flaw in the design. Fiction, the old volumes of literature stored in the library, was clearly marked as such. To deliberately publish things that were untrue? It was censurable. However, stamping words in ink on some non-electronic sheet, and stashing it behind a wall panel at that, stretched the bounds of what could be considered publication. An uneasy feeling crept up, and a word sprang to mind: sabotage.

No, now Dase was getting worked up, trying to find connections to explain something that didn't feel right. Their coping mechanism came to mind like a mantra: *name the pattern, break it, and change your mental scenery so you can relax.*

Dase needed to move around and put the conundrum out of mind. They slid on their mask and went outside. The air was crackling, oppressive. They could tell the atmosphere was getting out of sync, the Meteorology people would have to do an intervention soon. Weather events were always scheduled and announced at least a day in advance, but Dase never checked. They liked the feeling of intuiting when they were coming. Other people on the block didn't seem to notice. A dozen were out enjoying the hot, bright day.

Keeping their distance, Dase made their way to the Green. Colorful bunting had been stretched between the taller bushes. The pole stood in the middle.

"What's the theme?" they asked a neighbor seated on a bench.

"May Day. It's a Scandinavian tradition." The neighbor tossed out the phrase like it was a truly interesting bit of information, though the careful way they pronounced the word suggested they could not quite remember, from cursory geography lessons long faded in time, where exactly on Terra Scandinavia had been.

Dase nodded, recalling something about a dance, flowers, white dresses, colorful lengths of cloth wrapped around a pole. They wondered if they'd feel up for it, the day the block party came around. The air seemed to pulse angrily. They nodded and turned around.

Some days, Dase enjoyed spontaneous socializing, but today was not one of them. The regulation distance, the superficial topics, their neighbors' pleasant apathy, all of it got on their nerves.

Walking back to their module, they heard raised voices from one of the family units. That was unusual. The modules were effectively soundproofed: someone must really be shouting. Screaming, in fact. The sound was faint, but the tone was unmistakable. Not the low growl of anger, but the high shriek of desperation. Dase stopped, looking at the door, four down from their own. Another neighbor passed by, homeward, head down, politely giving them all the berth they could, since Dase was standing in the middle of the street. A minute later another neighbor passed the other way. No one acknowledged the screaming.

Trembling a bit in the pit of their stomach, Dase drew themself up and headed for the door. Someone wasn't alright, screaming like that. They should check in, at least offer some help. Just as they raised their hand to buzz, an electronic warble sounded from the direction of the Green. It was a safety drone, whirring agilely past the maypole and down the street.

"Please return to your modules. A therapeutic intervention is inbound."

Dase backed away from the safety drone, which took up a position at the door. The bitterness of early panic welling up from the pit of their stomach, they backed away. The drone repeated its admonition, and Dase retreated a little farther.

Farther down, Module opened their own door invitingly, but Dase could not bring themself to surrender the street just yet.

They caught the gentle sound of a klaxon from the far end of the block, and a moment later glimpsed a sled and two medics coming out of the health center. They had trouble getting the sled past the Green, what with the benches, the maypole, and a parked container, probably full of decorations for the upcoming festivities. One of them spoke a command and they pulled the pole out, quickly and efficiently laying it on the ground beside the benches.

A warm body pressed against Dase's ankle. They looked down to see Snookums, rubbing anxiously.

"I know, sweetie. It's scary." They rubbed the cat along its cheeks, mouth to ear, and it exuded appreciation.

The medics were at the family unit now. The door opened up and they went inside, followed by the drone. A minute later, they came out, supporting one of Dase's neighbors between them, one half of a couple Dase did not know so well; they had never kept a social appointment, though Dase had seen them bubbling away in the middle of the crowd at block parties. The person had a wild, exhausted look, their eyes unfocused. The medics helped them onto the sled and strapped them in. The other neighbor came to the doorway, head bowed, eyes wide, exuding worry, embarrassment, and fear.

"We'll take good care of them," Dase heard a medic say. "If all goes well, in a week or two they can come back here."

The neighbor nodded uncertainly, looking at their module mate, who by now was somewhere else, eyes pasted on the sky.

"We'll send a therapist to evaluate you later in the day," the medic went on. "Just for secondary effects. Stay home and try to relax. You're arrenarred from all work assignments and social appointments until you get an all clear."

The medics and the sled set off, back towards the node. The safety drone flitted off once the neighbor went back in the module. The streets were empty.

Dase went in and had a long cry, cuddling Snookums on the couch. It happened every now and then: someone broke down. Interstellar travel was hard on the human psyche, and *Hermetica* was the first crew to ever do it. They had to learn as they went, designing the best, most supportive environment possible despite being trapped together in a crowded ship with scarce resources.

Once, when Dase was an adolescent, an older person who worked as an instructor had a break down and had to be transported out of the school by an emergency team. It was an important moment for Dase, because of the group counseling that came afterwards. The instructor heard voices that other people could not hear, they had been told by therapists who came to talk to them and help them process the troubling event. Some kids in their cohort had snickered, even though it was strongly discouraged to mock or disparage the mental state of other passengers. *Encourage your fellow passengers' coping mechanisms, create a mutually supportive environment, and only report those behaviors and views that might enable sabotage*, those were the watch words as far as mental health was concerned.

What had been so important for Dase was to hear acknowledgment that someone could have different perceptions than those around them, that even though such difference could be problematic, it was something that happened to people. The fact that therapists could speak about divergent experiences in a soothing way helped Dase understand the stark, unmentionable differences they had been perceiving between themself and their peers.

From there, it was only a few more steps to realize that maybe what they experienced was legitimate, could even be healthy if there were a way to integrate it with the experiences and perceptions of their cohort.

What had the instructor been shouting? "We should tell them! We should tell them!" Maybe if they had been able to share what the voices had been saying, they never would have had a breakdown. But that was an optimistic view. That instructor never returned, meaning they had never been able to reintegrate. They had been submitted to a permanent reconciliation process. *Hermetica* tried to take care of all its passengers, but some simply could not cope. Perhaps the dominant, unspoken view was accurate: it was the weakest passengers who broke down, and though they all needed to support one another, in the end the only ones who would arrive at their destination were those who were fit to.

Dase could be pretty sure their genes would not be used in any of the restock cohorts that would make up *Hermetica*'s future generations. They wondered how much longer they could last. When would a medic team and a safety drone show up at their door?

Half an hour later Zimp called. Dase washed their face and turned on the screen.

"So how have you been?"

"Fine."

Zimp pursed their lips. "You sure?"

"Yeah, you know. Ups and downs."

"Anything interesting at work?"

"Oh, I got a patient in Meteo, they told me about plants."

"That's cool. Have you been looking at the plants on your block?"

"I guess. No more than usual."

"But you've been interested in the ship, right? Or the journey?"

"I'm just... having doubts."

"It's normal. You know that, right?"

"Yeah."

"They say that psychologically, our generation has it the hardest. We never saw Terra, we probably won't see the next homeworld. We're stuck yearning for two places that are completely unknown to us."

"Yeah."

"So don't be hard on yourself, is what I mean. It's okay if you feel down or directionless. The system was made to take that into account. Take as many personal days as you need."

"Personal days don't help!" Dase surprised themself with the feelings that came up.

Zimp blinked, afraid they'd said the wrong thing.

"I mean, it's *Hermetica*. It doesn't feel right. It feels like... nowhere."

"What do you mean?"

"I don't know. I mean, Terra, it had all this history, all these things happening. Most of them terrible, yeah. But here... I can't just spend my life waiting for the next block party."

"There's a lot more than block parties."

Dase shrugged.

"You're not gaming, are you?"

"I got sick of it."

"There's some really good ones..."

"I don't want to hear about it," they cut Zimp off. "Look, I'm not bored, I just... this doesn't feel real."

Zimp raised an eyebrow. "How's that?"

"Like... traveling through space, leaving the solar system, on our way to another star. That's amazing! I'd love to be a part of that!"

"You are."

"I don't think I am."

Zimp paused, taken aback. "What do you mean?"

"None of it feels real."

"Do you think... you could explain some more?"

Dase could see that Zimp was troubled by all this, and they felt bad. They had gone too far, dumping weight on someone else's shoulders. No one else could solve their problems for them. They tried to fix it. Zimp was a practical person. What was a way to describe their feeling that would present Zimp with a path towards solving it? A path away from the boundless despair Dase had opened up? It was an abyss that Zimp would be compelled to build a bridge over, could never, ever stare down into.

An answer appeared, and already the feeling slipped away, digging itself into a deeper territory.

"Look, I never got to take an advanced education, I never got into the stuff you and all the others got into. I feel like... I feel like I've never even been able to touch *Hermetica*, to be a part of the ship. Does that make sense? I need to ground myself, you know?"

"Yeah," Zimp said, face brightening. "So how do you do that?"

"I tried to find schematics of Hermetica, but they're off limits."

"Of course. Compartmentalization, enteekay. What do you need the schematics for?"

"I don't even know where on the ship I am. I've only seen the tiniest part of it."

"Well, I know I've seen more than you, but still, I haven't even seen 2% of the whole thing. But that's the New Safety for you. If the ship's population has a high interconnectivity, trouble spreads fast."

"How do we even know the ship is as big as they say?" Dase blurted out. "How do we know we're even going anywhere?"

Zimp rocked backwards. "That sounds paranoid."

Dase set their jaw.

"I'm sorry, I mean... We know *Hermetica*'s huge. There's millions of people on board, you can talk to all of them, get to know all of them."

Dase supposed it was true, though they had never excelled, like the others in their cohort, at making friends over a screen. In fact, the only people they had ever called, the only ones they would consider friends, they had met in person.

"You know what, I have an idea," Zimp offered. "You say you need to feel grounded?"

Dase nodded.

"I can whip up, just for you, a special science experiment."

"Yeah?"

"What would you say if I told you I could give you the chance to take a look at *Hermetica*?"

"You'd be my hero!"

"Obviously, I can't get you a permit to go to an observation window or take a space walk, but I can let you see the spinning of the giant platform we're on right now."

"Do I get to be your student for a day?"

"Even better! My students do most of the syllabus through simulations, but you and I, we can do something hands on. I'm not allowed to take materials out of the lab, but I bet..." Zimp's head was turning this way and that, looking about their own module, off camera "...I can find all the supplies I need for a simple experiment."

"Tell me about it!" Dase pleaded.

"You'll have to do some homework to understand what you'll see."

"I promise!"

"So we're on a giant platform, attached to a ring that's spinning around *Hermetica*'s core."

"I know, I know."

"Right. That's what generates the pseudogravity that keeps

us in place. But we can detect the Coriolis force that correlates with our rotation."

"Okay," Dase said uncertainly. They understood the principles that Zimp was describing, but not how it would allow them to see *Hermetica*.

Their friend picked up on their skepticism. "What that means is, if the experiment works, you'll be able to tell which way our platform is rotating, you'll be able to look up in to the sky and visualize the axis of that rotation, which in this case is the core of *Hermetica* itself, and you'll be able to tell which way we're heading. What do you say to that?"

"That would be wonderful!"

Zimp looked around again. "Well, I need to make sure I can design this thing so the results will actually be visible to the naked eye," they chuckled. "The rings have really low rpm, and I don't want to let you down! So I'm going to get to work on that... I wonder if I can get my hands on some ball bearings... but, I'm going to send you some materials, a little light reading on inertial forces to get you up to speed, pardon the joke."

"Same time tomorrow?" Dase asked.

"Sure, I'll try to have it ready."

"You're such a sweetheart!"

"Nice to see you smile."

It's true, Dase realized as the screen went black. They were smiling.

The next morning, Dase doubled their exercise routine and then went in to see some patients. The air on the block broiled and rippled, neighbors walked by oblivious. At the health center, they saw the botanist and a developer, a regular. Their sessions dragged on. Dase's mind was elsewhere. The patients didn't seem to notice.

Back at the module, Dase downed an emmery, then called up another one, ate that too. Fidgeted a while. Went to the Green, sat on a bench beneath the colored bunting, and tried reading. It was an archaic work, full of obsolete pronouns and strange social relationships Dase had a hard time following, conflicts that didn't seem to make any sense at all. This one was about a person named Edna who spent all their day in idleness. First on vacation, now with one lover, now with another, but never happy with anything. It described a society in which everyone seemed to be perpetually running away from one another, and at the same time, chained together.

Dase put the novel down. The air had become a solid thing. What was the conflict in the story? Was Edna just a weak, fatuous person? That wouldn't make for an interesting tale. Amidst the nebulous anxieties the novel plotted, Dase perceived the outlines of another character, unnamed, invisible yet ever present, filling Edna and all the others with dread. Oppressive and everywhere at once, like the heat that day.

Were there video cameras at the time this novel was written? Dase didn't think so. That might explain the fear of being seen all the characters seemed to display, but they were sure the novel predated video cameras by half a century. They lifted the portable again, intrigued. Léonce came back into the narrative. Dase didn't understand that character at all. They seemed to have no connection whatsoever with Edna, and yet they were bound. Léonce decided where Edna's children should go, at one point they spoke with a doctor about what should be done with Edna, without Edna even being present, but most of the time they were just somewhere else. Did Léonce possess some magical power over Edna? The story made no mention of magic, but perhaps they were supposed to intuit its existence. Primitive literature was often strange like that.

The stiffness of the air continued to build. *Hermetica* produced a lot of heat. Surely it could not hold. And there it was: the first wisp of movement. It would all come falling down now. Already was falling, even if no one else noticed.

Now the story was getting interesting. Edna was speaking with a musician, a pianist. They had a nice relationship, one that made a little more sense, and the pianist did not seem to be afraid of whomever it was that terrified everyone else so much.

Another lick of air ruffled Dase's hair. An alert popped up in the corner of the screen. They tapped on it. A pihessay: *Meteorology has fast-tracked an atmospheric adjustment for this afternoon. The scheduled precipitation event has been upgraded to a Class 3 adjustment. Citizens are advised to remain in their modules, starting at 18 aitch.*

Dase grinned from ear to ear. Called it.

There was still another hour before the call with Zimp. An eternity. They suddenly lost their patience with the novel.

"Portable, is there an open slot for a jog?" It wasn't easy to get a slot on short notice, but in this heat, it was possible. Not many other people were out on the block.

"There's a fifteen minute slot opening up in six minutes. Is that acceptable?"

"Book it!"

Dase went back to the module, changed into track clothes, and went out the door. Keeping a good pace, they went around the block—the full cross—ten times. Four kilometers. The portable beeped in paternal consternation a few times on the last lap, they had exceeded their slot, but no one else was showing up to run. Back in their module, they stripped and threw the clothes in the chute. The shower extracted and they stepped in, cold water making them gasp in exhilaration.

Once they'd had enough time to get soaked twice over and relish the chill just a little longer, the module chimed in. "Shall I switch to hot now?"

"Right on time."

Soon the air was steaming, and Dase leaned against the tiled wall in bliss. "Can I get another liter? Just steam?"

"You're close to your limit."

"I'll skip tomorrow. Just give me another liter. Please?"

The tight stream of aerated water toggled to a focused bath of steam, and Dase felt time slip away. When it was finally over, they moved at an indolent pace, toweling off and leisurely picking new clothes as the shower vacked itself and retracted.

Just a few minutes remained before Zimp's call. Dase opened the article they had sent, scanning through it on their portable. They kept the wall screen free, black like infinite potential. The article was a useful refresher, all things they had studied before the aptitudes.

The image of the examiner popped into their head, the screen at the front of the class, the tension of a ticking clock, a diminishing block of time, and so many questions, too many to answer, all of them... pointing to the future? Or closing the way?

They had gotten through half the article. Zimp still hadn't called. Dase looked up at the wall screen. Nothing, just blackness.

"Message Zimp. Are we still on? Experiment giving you problems? Lemme know if you want to postpone."

They went back to reading. Three minutes later, and there was no reply.

"Call Zimp."

"Zimp is unavailable," Module said after a short pause.

"Unavailable? Like, out of the module without their

portable?" Dase could imagine no other form of unavailability. One could always turn off calls, of course, but that simply routed calls straight to message.

"There's a block."

"A block?" Dase wasn't even sure what that meant.

"Please wait."

Now things were downright strange. They wished Snookums were here.

"Module, what's…"

"Please wait."

Was Module frozen? It had never happened before, but it was feasible. Maybe a programming upgrade had caused some functions to go offline. They wondered if that meant they were stuck inside. They were just about to go to the door when the buzzer rang.

Dase jumped. And then, because they could find no explanation for the feeling of dread that boiled through them, they opened the door.

A person they had never seen before, a bit older, with stern eyes, walked in.

"Hello Dase. Sorry for intruding like this. I'm Emel. I'm a block rep. May I take my mask off?"

Dase made a gesture of polite assent. "What's going on?" Their mouth went dry as they spoke.

"I'm sorry to inform you, we've temporarily blocked your communications."

"Oh… is that what happened. Um… why?"

"You were flagged for circumventing some of the compartmentalization protocols that are integral to the New Safety. I'm sure it was an innocent mistake on your part, but I need to give you an evaluation just to make sure no further procedures are needed."

"What… what did I do?"

"You were about to participate in an unauthorized experiment that might have enabled the collection of sensitive information about *Hermetica* in violation of Need to Know."

"Oh, the... the Coriolis thing?"

"That's right," Emel replied with a patient smile.

"How is that a violation?"

"I know it must seem like an innocent inquiry, something that would fall under the hobbies statute, but unfortunately, only citizens working in Physics are allowed to take measurements related to acceleration, or even the axis of rotation for the life platforms. You understand why we need to compartmentalize, with no exceptions. Remember the *Wiki*."

How could Dase forget the *Wiki*? The history was drilled into the heads of every young cohort on the ship. The *Wiki* was *Hermetica*'s sister ship. The two had departed at the same time, heading for the same cluster of stars, with the same objective: find and colonize a new homeworld. But they had been designed according to radically different models. There had been a strong debate in the space program, and in the spirit of openness and scientific inquiry, the Terran governments that ran the program agreed to let proponents of the two top models each have a free hand in designing their ships. The *Wiki* was designed according to a completely open source model, with every passenger given full access to all the information and permission to rewrite code and tweak design. It was billed as a constantly self-correcting work in progress that made maximum usage of the full intellectual resources of the passengers.

And it worked well for the first few years, with *Wiki* passengers developing a number of propulsion and life support innovations that *Hermetica* quickly adopted. But as the two ships approached Pluto's orbit, communication cut out. One final transmission warned of an attempted takeover, with reports of fighting on the *Wiki*, and then the entire ship exploded. No one would ever know who the saboteurs were, if they were terrorists or engineers with cabin fever, if there had been a power struggle between different factions trying to impose their design for the ship.

All they knew was the mantra, repeated in classrooms across *Hermetica* after the sociopsychs ran it through their simulations and confirmed the systemic flaw: "Open source systems are vulnerable to sabotage by disciplined and determined parties. Centralization and compartmentalization are the best way to prevent anarchic power struggles."

"So," Dase asked, "we can't do our Coriolis experiment?"

"I'm afraid not. And Dase? I need you to tell me what's going on."

"What do you mean?" Their palms got clammy.

"Your line of questioning, your reasoning for wanting to do the experiment... the recommendation is for a psych evaluation. And you were already flagged the day before for damage to your module."

They knew about the wall panel. Of course they knew. So did they already know what they had discovered? If they did, hiding it would only make things worse. Dase went to get the strange sheet.

"I found this. In the wall."

The rep pursed their lips as they gripped the sheet, fingers like tweezers. Their look darkened as they scanned the contents of the two articles.

"And I imagine you're quite confused."

"I am. It talks about things that don't make sense. Things that don't add up."

"And that's why you wanted to do an experiment?"

"Well the experiment was Zimp's idea. They don't know anything about the articles," they rushed to add. "But I was feeling... estranged. Reading all those things about Terra. You know I did poorly on the aptitudes—"

"You did well on the aptitudes," Emel interrupted, "you simply got tracked to an assignment that perhaps you no longer find satisfying."

"Okay. But what I mean to say is, I've never gotten to work on a system that's an integral part of *Hermetica*. Yes, I know," Dase headed off the next interruption, "*the human passengers are the most integral system of all, and palliative therapy is a vital part of the whole,*" Dase recited the pihessays dryly. But *Hermetica*, it feels unreal for me."

The rep did not look pleased with that answer. "And why did this sheet exacerbate that feeling?"

"It talks about a virus on Earth. On Terra. The choking sickness. How could the same virus have struck on Terra and on *Hermetica*?"

"We don't know the article refers to the same virus," the rep explained patiently. "It could simply be a similar one. Maybe an ancestral strain was already dormant in human populations when *Hermetica* set out, and similar, virulent strains evolved in both places. Without a comparative genetic analysis, who's to say?"

"Yeah, but, how did an article from Terra about things that happened after we already left wind up aboard the ship? The sheet's non-electronic, it didn't get beamed here."

The rep held their silence a moment. A vein on their neck fluttered and bulged. "Just because a piece of paper contains a bit of information, doesn't mean it's true. I appreciate that you have many questions that seem valid to you. I also appreciate that, when faced with a doubt, you had the discretion to not go immediately onto your socials and begin spreading it throughout the ship. Nonetheless, certain inquiries, when they go beyond idle curiosity, to achieve a satisfactory answer, require scientific exploration, as you know. Unfortunately, our safety demands a compartmentalized approach to avoid putting sensitive information in the open. *Trust in the experts, but let everyone become an expert,*" Emel repeated the old motto. "Of course, no one person can become an expert in everything. That's impossible. People have to stick to their field, or they risk confusing everybody."

"So... what are you saying?"

"You've found an intriguing piece of a puzzle, I'll give you that. But you're not the only one."

"I'm not?"

"No, Dase, you're not. Everyone else is working on the same puzzle. The physicists are working on propulsion, the biologists are working on life support systems, the designers are working on quality and entertainment, my team works on safety, and all of us are working together on the greatest mystery of all, how to sustainably project human life into the stars. I play my role and you play yours."

Something they had said stuck with Dase. "You... work in Safety? I thought you were an interblock rep?"

Emel's jaw clenched again. "They're overlapping fields. Sometimes we have to work together. Now listen to me. You can stick to your assignments and your social circuits. If you feel that your curiosity is related to a capacity that can be trained and put to *Hermetica*'s use, I can arrange for you to retake the aptitudes. And if you feel like these restrictions are unfair, you can enter into a reconciliation."

"A reconciliation with whom?" Dase asked. "Who have I harmed?"

"A reconciliation with the ship's Agreements," the rep replied tersely.

Dase nodded. They could tell arguing would only make things worse.

The rep left a short time later. The communications block would be removed after a short period of observation, they had said. They confiscated the sheet with the two articles, what had they called it? The *paper*.

Dase felt wrecked. Like they were surrounded with nowhere to go. The confines of the module were oppressive. "Tattle tale," they growled. It was too much. They wanted to smash the screen, to yank out all the wall panels, to pull out the bed and rip off the sheets, to call up emmeries and throw them on the floor. The austere face of the examiner came to mind. The damned aptitudes, circumscribing their future. This damn block rep, or whoever they were. It wasn't fair. They had to move, they had to go somewhere.

Fortunately, the door opened and let them out into the street. The air was heavy and damp. As they walked towards the Green, boiling, the first drops began to fall. Fat, heavy, cold drops of rain. A precipitation event, when all the specialists couldn't get humidity optimally distributed across the ship, and they had to flood a few blocks with a downpour. With all their systems, all their modeling, all their aptitudes, the experts still could not work out the unexpected, the chaotic.

Dase laughed at them as the rain fell harder. A sudden flash made them jump, a major electrostatic discharge ripping across the sky. But was it in the sky, the projection, or was the flash real, a bolt of charged particles equalizing from one end of the platform to the other? They could give no answer. All they could do was look upwards, face full of rain, and wait for another one.

And it came, and they felt the light run through them.

Now they were at the Green, and the rain was falling so hard it filled their eyes and soaked their clothes. No one else was out. Unthinkable. All the cameras were blinded by the thick sheets of rain. Not even a drone could fly in this downpour. Dase was completely alone. And they danced.

The world opened up to them. The shrubs swayed and trembled, the bunting drooped and broke, the benches splattered and endured, and Dase danced, generous leaping and joyous pirouettes, their arms outstretched, taking everything, as though there were no end to what could be given, and offering all of themself in return. They were doing loops around the maypole now, bouncing, spinning circles of endless return.

More lightning flashed. The rain pounded on the street like a stampede, the street was full, Dase and a million feet, arriving, always arriving, endless.

Dase was panting. Never had they run so hard. Their mouth was full of rain. Their hair was a river. The rain was in their belly button, in the crack of their ass, on their eyelashes, between their toes. They could hear the world breathing.

As the paroxysm eased, Dase found themself wandering around the block. Everything was newly acquainted, not a single meter of darkened, water-slick street was one they had walked down before, spent years walking down. These streets belonged to them tonight.

When the last drizzle subsided, Dase returned to their module. They shed their soaking clothes and went straight to the far wall. Module, surprised, reacted late. The bed extracted after they'd already arrived, waiting for it. Had they been expected to towel off first? Now they too were a part of the unexpected, a wisp of storm broken off, unvanquished. They smiled fiercely as they dripped into the sheets, riding on rising cumulae of dreams.

In the morning, they knew. Emel had been lying. All of them had been lying. They walked straight out the door, unclothed, fast unbroken, leaving Module in the middle of a sentence. They walked up and down the street, looking at the modules, the sky. They did not have Zimp's knack for equations, but surely they could find something. A proof.

But all there was were two cross streets and four nodes. No other way out. What had the rep said their choices were? Keep to their circuits, retake the aptitudes, or a reconciliation? No. They were lying. There were always other choices. The smaller units were three meters high, with a rounded lip and no handhold on the façade. No way a single person could get on top of one. But Dase was not a single person. They were a million feet. They were a storm cloud.

As neighbors avoided their gaze and hurried onward towards destinations, Dase found themself in front of the maypole.

"Hello, dancing partner," they smiled.

The maypole kept on, pointing towards the sky.

"Yeah, you're the one, aren't you? You'll take me where I need to go. Now if I can just get you to change position..."

They knew it was possible. They had seen it done. All they needed was an accomplice. Dase could only imagine what sort of blocks they had on them, all throughout the system by now.

A neighbor was rushing along to one of the nodes, studiously avoiding Dase's nakedness.

"You," they said. "Stop."

Terrified, the neighbor complied. Dase smiled.

"We need to clear the way for a therapeutic intervention. Tell the block to release this element so we can move it out of the way."

Clearly uncomfortable, but seduced by the logic that a therapeutic intervention was, indeed, in order, the neighbor stepped forward and said in a trembling voice, "Block, uh, we need you to, uh, release this pole."

Dase could almost sense the hesitation. Clearly all kinds of models and algorithms were telling the block this was a terrible idea. But human overrides were given a backdoor precisely for those situations in which the system did not understand which criteria to prioritize. The block relented, and the ground panel released its hold on the maypole.

"Thanks!" Dase said pleasantly. "You can go."

They got a grip on the pole and lowered it down onto their shoulder. It actually didn't weigh that much, despite its height, and they were able to drag it off the Green. The day was going perfectly so far.

A klaxon sounded in the direction of the health center, but Dase didn't care. They were humming, they couldn't remember what song. Arriving at a single person unit, Dase propped the pole against the edge of the roof. It leaned in at an angle that was somewhat steeper than $45°$, but still not so steep that they couldn't shimmy up it. And shimmy they did!

The medics arrived then, running towards them, but they were most of the way up and the medics were afraid to dislodge the pole and cause Dase to fall.

"Hello!" they called. And then they were at the roof. "Goodbye!"

The roof was the same color and texture as the façade. The most remarkable thing about it was, once they walked in a couple meters, the street disappeared. They were in a completely new place, all their own: not in a module, out of doors, but not under the watchful eyes of the street. But they weren't out yet.

The adjoining module, a family unit, was two meters taller. They were able to gain the roof with a running jump. Now they were higher than they'd ever been in their life, and the next destination was already in reach. The module's roof connected with a broad platform, the roof for the life support and storage facilities that filled up each of the four corners of the block. They ran thirty odd meters, and then they were at the wall. The wall that they had never seen, but always intuited, marking the outer boundary between this block and the next. And it was only a meter higher than the roof where they now stood.

Dase was nervous. They had not known what they would find here. In theory, every block was walled off on all six sides, and the only way in or out was through a node. There was a transparent membrane under the sky that allowed for the controlled circulation of air and water. But Dase didn't know if the membrane came all the way down to the top of the physical wall, forming a pocket around each block, if they could detach the membrane or tear it.

It turned out to be even easier. There must have been a substantial gap, because Dase could not see or feel any membrane as they climbed up on the wall. And just like that, they had gotten out of the block. They had made their own choice, their own way out.

Dase started to run. The top of the wall was broad and flat, and running was easy. They ran fast, they ran far. They didn't know how many blocks they left behind, and they kept running. The sun was bright and glorious. The wind blew freely. It was all connected, unobstructed. They were sure of that now. A cumulus cloud swelled up, cast them into shadow. Their skin cooled. The cloud moved on, and immediately, the heat and light returned. Tears came to their eyes. *The sun was majestic, undeniable. The wind went wherever it pleased. All the colors unfolded themselves from the blue and blinding white.*

The wall continued as far as they could see. Every hundred meters they came to an intersection where another wall, perpendicular, stretched right and left, making the horizon in both directions. But they knew the grid was not unending. Because when they strained to look into that farthest distance, the horizon curled down, not *up*, but *down!* They were in a different place entirely. Their tears flowed freely.

The wall passed over another node. How many blocks had they run past now? Their world had grown infinitely larger. This time, they veered off to the side. A gentle whirring accompanied them from behind. Now they were running atop modules again, peering over the edge into the street of an unknown block, it might as well have been a foreign country. People were in the street, strangers. They looked up in astonishment.

"The sky is real!" Dase cried at them. "The sky is real!"

The whirring came closer.

Dase ran on to another block, atop the modules overlooking another street. Now they were sobbing uncontrollably. Joyous, broken. "The sky is real! The sky is real!"

No one knew what to make of the crazy prophet on the rooftops. They didn't have to think about it long.

The safety drones caught up to Dase. Four milliamps of current, pushed through their skin and into a circuit of muscle and bone by 50,000 volts of electromotive force, and they were on the ground.

2

DASE CAME TO IN PIECES, AS THE SEDATIVES WORE OFF. Their hands started working first, probing in amusement at body parts that were alienated, unfeeling, not yet plugged back in to the neuralgic network. *What's this,* the hands seemed to say, *a leg, a pelvis, genitals, placed right within arms reach. To whom does it belong?*

Dase laughed along with their hands. Who had left a leg there? What their hands were doing, they could not say. They were not yet present enough to feed them a purpose, the hands seemed to have a purpose of their own, why should Dase be telling the hands what to do?

There was a sudden tingling, not entirely pleasant. Was that, was that leg Dase's leg? Oh. Why were fingers poking at their leg?

Dase was back at the office.

No. No, that wasn't true. There was a plexi on one side. There was a plexi on the other side. There were plexis on every side. Where were their instruments? This wasn't the office. Dase tried to sit up.

Dase came to in pieces, as the sedatives wore off. First their eyes opened. Their head didn't feel great. Their stomach didn't either. Their legs were tingling uncomfortably. Their hands seemed to be asleep.

There was a memory. The sky. A tear formed in their left eye. Where were they? They sat up, slowly. It was some kind of holding cell.

A metallic column in one corner pinged. A small door, flush with the column's curve, slid open. A cup of water was revealed within. Dase drank it down. They replaced the cup. The door closed. A moment later, it opened again. The cup was full. Dase drank.

There was a toilet in the far corner. Dase sat down. The plexis phased opaque. It took a while, but finally they were able to piss. They staggered back to the bed. The plexis went transparent again. The column pinged. The door opened. There was a tray of food this time. An emmery, in principle, but different from any emmery they'd eaten. They felt weak, they wanted the food, but their stomach roiled as they ate. They lay back down on the cot.

When Dase awoke, there was a person on the other side of the plexi. They wore strange clothes of a thick material, plaid red on top, blue bottoms, and their skin was as pasty as John Wayne's. The person was eyeing Dase suspiciously.

"You up?"

In response, Dase pulled themself into a sitting position. "Hi." Their voice croaked, and their head spun a little. They rubbed their temples until the feeling passed.

"Just get in?"

"Um, I guess so."

"They sedate newcomers. Me, I've been here a while, but they transferred me from another block."

Dase looked around to see walls on all six sides. The four lateral sides were transparent plexi. Two had breathing holes and looked out on the narrow corridors that flanked the cell. The other two looked into cells just like the one they occupied. The person with the funny clothes was in a cell.

"I'm Dase."

"That's your name?"

Dase nodded. What a strange person.

"Robert."

"Nice to meet you."

Robert let out a quiet snort, but they smiled amiably.

Dase peered around. Between the lighting and the way the block was built, they couldn't see if anyone was in the cells across the corridor, nor how far down the corridors extended.

"You're not from around here, are you?"

Dase remembered what they had discovered, running atop the wall fleeing from their block. None of it seemed real anymore. Could it be possible? Such a big lie?

"I guess not. Where are we?"

"Got me there."

Dase hesitated. "Is this... *Hermetica*?"

"Where's that? East Coast?"

Robert did not know what *Hermetica* was.

"To be honest, I'm not exactly sure."

Robert scrunched up their face.

"What about you. Where are you from?"

"Oregon."

Oregon, East Coast. Those sounded like Terran references. It was too much evidence to deny. The articles from 2023, from Terra, mentioning the pandemic and nothing about extrasystem travel. The block on their communication when they were about to measure the Coriolis force. The realness of the sky. The view from atop the wall, not consistent with a concave, curving platform.

Hermetica had never left. They had been on Terra the whole time. Could it be possible? The magnitude of the lie was dizzying. Dase craved confirmation. But how to ask without sounding completely bizarre? They needed more information.

"What's Oregon like?" they asked innocently.

"Our community's nice. Peaceful, no crime, all God-fearing men and women. We've got fifty thousand acres, timber, corn, potatoes, we bring in a good crop."

Robert had a strange way of speaking. Nonetheless, they understood most of it, and none of it sounded like life on a spaceship, not any ship that Dase could imagine. But they wanted to make sure.

"Do you have mountains?"

"Mountains? You bet we do."

"Have you been to the sea?"

"The Pacific? I've been there, but I don't travel much."

Mountains, an ocean. It would be quite a feat to get those on a ship. That settled it. Unless Robert were lying—and they could not guess what motive the other prisoner might have for such a bizarre lie—they were on Terra. They had always been on Terra. None of them were going to colonize a new homeworld. None of them would ever get there.

"Tell me, Dase, you're not from the Secession, are you?"

"The Secession?"

"Oh boy. The Secession? The Second Civil War? Do they not teach you people about any of that?"

"Sorry," Dase shrugged.

"The fake virus? The totalitarian coup? None of that ring a bell?"

"We had a virus..."

"You think you did. I'm sorry to break it to you, but where you grew up, that's a totalitarian society. They made a fake virus to try to keep everyone locked up. But patriots fought back and we won our independence. Took half the country with us. Honestly I'm not surprised they don't teach you about us."

"Yeah, I guess... there's a lot of things they didn't teach us." The line about a fake virus reminded Dase of something in one of the articles.

"You seem alright, even if you are from the other side. How'd you end up here? What'd you do, cross the border?"

"I was... running. I went over the wall."

"Yeah, we don't take too kindly to people going over that wall. But don't you worry. I'm sure they'll send you back in no time. And when they do, you make sure you tell your people about what really happened. There never was any virus."

"So, we're in the Secession now?" Dase's head was reeling. Their grasp on what was fact and what was fiction had already been seriously loosened, and their interlocutor in the next cell didn't exactly inspire confidence. It was not the oily feel of a well designed lie that Emel had emitted, but rather the blind self-assurance that whatever happened to be most convenient was an unquestionable truth. That was the impression Dase got, and now they knew better than to discount their intuition.

"Don't know where else we'd be," Robert shrugged matter of factly. They looked around at the plexi walls. "Though this is definitely not our local jail. Tell you the truth, I don't like it one bit. No lawyer, no phone call. This is how I imagine jail looks like outside the Secession. Didn't think we were supposed to have facilities like this. For illegals, sure. But for citizens? Maximum security, I suppose." They chuckled, showing an ironic pride Dase failed to understand.

"So, how'd you get in here?""

"I shot a man," Robert said plainly.

"Oh." Dase struggled to fathom exactly what that would mean. Neuromuscular incapacitation, infection prone puncture wounds, uncontrollable nausea, irradiation, dismemberment, fatal blood loss... They decided against inquiring after the technology level of ranged weapons in the Secession. Besides, Robert's vocabulary was thoroughly quaint, and Dase wasn't sure they'd understand anyway.

"And you don't know when you'll get out?"

"Nope. I've barely seen any guards, definitely haven't spoken to any officials, not since the sheriff turned me over to those marshals. This place is high tech, I tell you that. Practically runs itself. First I was in a block with other people from the Secession. Then they just moved me. Honestly, you're the first person I've seen from the outside. I mean, not counting when I'm on border patrol. But we don't talk much with the illegals when we see 'em," he choked back a laugh. "Don't you worry, though, we only shoot the bad ones. The good ones, the ones looking for freedom, Christians who are being persecuted, we give them a chance if they work hard. Asylum, you know. There are plenty of communities that would take in someone like you. But our community's a bit special, lot of veterans from the war, so we get final say on who moves in and well, you, you wouldn't exactly fit in." Robert chuckled, pointing at Dase as though it were self-evident. Dase nodded like they understood.

The day wore on. They ate when the next food tray arrived. Dase decided not to confide in Robert about *Hermetica*. Robert was condescending enough already, and Dase did not want to give them any ammunition.

They thought about their friends. How many of them knew the truth? It was possible that none of them did. They trusted Zimp absolutely. They wouldn't lie to Dase. They had grown up together. In fact, Zimp had been helping them get a better sense for their place on *Hermetica*. Someone from Safety had probably paid them a visit before they could carry out the experiment. Dase wondered how Zimp would have reacted. And somehow, they knew. The Safety team member, they would have said Dase had suffered a mental breakdown. That they were becoming obsessed, denying the reality of the situation. And that, even though Zimp's intentions were good, catering to that paranoia—they would call it a paranoia—was only encouraging the behavior. Then Zimp would receive a reminder to help uphold the New Safety and not spread Need to Know information, whatever set up they'd put together to carry out the experiment would be confiscated. The next day at work they'd get a challenging new assignment that would keep them busy. When they checked, Dase would be classified as permanent reconciliation.

Would that be enough? Would Zimp make their peace and say goodbye, without ever knowing what had really happened to their old friend?

It seemed so absurd. They were so smart! How could they not know? But Dase remembered how they'd been educated. Plenty of formulae and equations, but all the experiments were done on simulations. They were asked to complete mathematical proofs, to test the technical knowledge they'd been given, but never to test the story of who they were, where they were, how they'd gotten there.

It was masterful misdirection. They'd been given the tools to take apart their world, all of them, but they'd also been given a more interesting project to put those tools to use on. So they put their shoulders to the wheel, and the world stood, unquestioned.

What about Emel, the putative interblock rep. Did they know? Dase assumed they did, surely Emel had actually been a Safety investigator. But the more they thought about how Zimp had been fooled, how they themself had been fooled, the more doubts appeared.

If Emel was willing to accept that their job consisted of protecting compartmentalization, of making sure no one tried obtaining knowledge outside of their professional assignment, of checking up on anyone flagged for abnormal behavior, and making a simple recommendation—whether that person could be trusted to follow the rules, whether they needed a temporary reconciliation process, or whether they presented a permanent danger—they really didn't need to know anything. All they had to tell themself was that sabotage was a threat to *Hermetica* and anyone violating compartmentalization was enabling sabotage. The articles, that for Dase had triggered so many questions, for Emel probably just tripped an alarm: unauthorized, sensitive information that had to be controlled.

Dase thought about how no one they knew worked in a field that gave them proof *Hermetica* existed. Sure, there was someone who worked in propulsion, but they were pretty sure that person just ran models on improving the efficiency of fusion reactions. They never would have seen the engines, and didn't know how their results were actually put to use. Everyone had such a small part of the picture, and it was the system itself that fed the bigger picture back to them. They all trusted that the information they produced was being put together in a sensible way.

As for the millions of passengers, who knew how many of them were real people? From what Dase had seen on their run, there were thousands for sure, all living and working in identical blocks covering at least 25km². Somewhere with a naturally flat terrain. But no one knew more than a couple hundred people for real. The majority of those millions who were active, visible, on socials, could have been artificials, there to confirm the alibi everyone was so intent on believing.

Dase felt sick. Most of all because on some level, it wasn't a surprise. That world had always felt empty.

Something moved just at the edge of their field of vision. Dase turned. Nothing. For a moment, they thought, hoped, it was Snookums. But Snookums couldn't find them here. Which was a tragedy, because they could use a good cuddle. They curled up on the cot.

"You got the blues?" Robert called.

Dase sat up and shrugged. They had been napping lightly, an oneiric distortion of the last days' revelations roiling through their head. They felt lethargic, like there wasn't any need to grab onto any one of the coherent versions of reality that suggested itself, like it didn't even matter.

"That happens. You gotta be patient in here."

They gave a compliant nod.

Robert mistook their silence for a request to force them into a state of cheerfulness. "This won't last forever. Soon you'll get to go back and be with your people."

Dase nodded again.

"I tell you what, I sure miss my wife."

Wife... wife... Dase remembered encountering the term in old literature. It was something along the lines of either a friend or a servant. Should they ask? They might as well indulge in their curiosity a little if Robert was going to make avoiding a conversation impossible.

"What do you miss about them?" Dase hoped the question was neutral enough that the answer would reveal the word's meaning.

"Who?"

"What?"

"Miss about who?"

"Your wife? You just said you missed them."

"I only got the one, we're not polygamists."

Now Dase was thoroughly confused. "Right. Your one wife. What do they do?"

"You mean *she*?" Robert looked at Dase like some insult had been proffered.

"*She*?" Dase vaguely remembered the word from some old novels that hadn't been translated into modern English, one of a class of obsolete pronouns.

Spurred on by Dase's blank look, Robert chortled. "She, he... you know?"

"Umm, okay."

"Are you telling me you don't say he and she?"

In an unguarded moment, Dase snapped back at Robert's scorn. "Well, they are archaic."

"Oh for crying out loud. I heard stories about this, but it had to be a tall tale! Don't tell me you people pretend men and women don't exist!"

This had taken an interesting turn. Dase figured they could either lay back down and put an end to the conversation, or make it a little less one-sided, given the likelihood that they would be stuck in it, willing or not, for the next several days. And finding out more about Robert's world might answer some questions they had about their own. "Well, it's certainly a classification system that once existed."

"A classifica- How are you going to deny what's in front of your very nose?"

Since crashing out on the aptitudes, Dase had not felt confident talking about scientific matters with their peers. Prior to that, though, they had been a voracious student. And in the short time they had known Robert, they had already chafed under their condescension. Dase was certainly a capable mind when compared to Robert. Maybe they were even intelligent when compared to *Hermetica*'s brightest, they realized, a blossom of warm confidence spreading through their chest. Of all the cohort mates they had been deferring to these last years of their life, who had been sent on to prestigious work assignments, none of them had been smart enough to figure out it was all a lie. It was time for Dase to start trusting in their hunches.

Robert presented an interesting challenge. Like running into a modern-day Aristotle and trying to explain how atomic theory was more practical than the notion of five elements. The objection Robert seemed to be raising was not terribly complex. The challenge consisted of fitting about two years of primary school rudimentaries into a single conversation. But it seemed like they had time. Dase clasped their hands and shifted into a posture that was neither confrontational nor dismissive, facing Robert but not quite head on.

"Have you thought about your approach? I don't know why you need to divide up the human species according to a classification system that goes beyond current functionality, I mean job descriptions. It seems like a dodgy enterprise. But if you're going to insist, maybe we can agree the fundamental feature of the system should be clarity? No room for ambiguity?"

Robert was taken aback by this sudden change in register, but they nodded all the same. "That's right. Clarity."

Dase continued. "Well on those grounds, it seems the notion of men and women would have to be rejected."

Robert sputtered.

"Chromosomatic difference is not binary, you were aware of that, right? Hormones, genital development, none of it is strictly binary. And it's dangerous to establish a biological generalization and shed the rest as a rounding error, because, well, those rounding errors are people. And as for the ones who supposedly fit in the boxes, there's an additional danger, as some will fit better than others. So now you have a non-utilitarian value hierarchy. Instead of just being human, everyone is now either more or less. Plus the fact that the distinction serves no purpose. So: ambiguous, problematic, and useless. Honestly, I don't think there's a systems analysis in existence that would class this metric as operational."

"It. Is. Self. Evident," Robert said lividly.

Standing up for themself, Dase had started feeling manic, and from there it was a short hop to cocky. Time for a tidy *coup de grâce*. "Oh yeah? Which one am I?"

"Woman," Robert said without blinking.

Dase had to hand it to them. They were unflinchingly bold to make a claim they knew, they both knew, they could not possibly back up.

"How do you know?" Dase stuttered.

"It's obvious," Robert drawled, as though it were, in fact, obvious.

"Well, you haven't given me a chromosome test. We just met."

"But it's, it's plain as day, anyone can see it."

"I don't see it."

"Because you're brainwashed." Robert rolled their eyes.

Now that certainly took the cake.

"And what are you, then?"

"Man," Robert shrugged, misunderstanding the question.

Dase rolled with it. "Have you ever taken a chromosome test?"

"Don't need to."

"Don't you think that's a self-confirming theory. If you never test it, you never have to find out if it's wrong."

Robert sighed like their patience was wearing thin. "Look at me. Now look at you."

"Yeah. We look quite different."

"Aha."

"Well, we're not close genetic relations, why should we look similar?"

"Okay, trying not to be indelicate. For starters, I have a beard."

"Yeah, so do I, look. A moustache, anyway. See? Right here?"

"You don't shave, I get that, it's gross. No need to flaunt it."

"But if people have to adapt their behavior and even modify their bodies to confirm the theory, then those are false metrics."

"Oh for the love of God! I can't have babies! You can have babies!"

"Well... you could have babies with the right surgical procedures." Here Robert's eyes widened alarmingly. "And neither of us know if I could, in fact, reproduce in my current state. I've never applied, never gotten tested. And even if I could, or even if I got the procedure to make sure I could, there would undoubtedly come a time in my life when it would no longer be an option. Would I then cease to be a woman?"

"Look, women can have babies, and barring some perverse voodoo science, men cannot."

Dase was feeling a bit offended. They rose to their feet. "It's a flimsy assumption to think that someone with no hair on their face has productive ovaries and a viable birth canal, and then on top of it to get disgusted with someone who doesn't shave their face because you insist on believing they can bear children. But beyond all that, childbearing is a bad metric for a social division, because it's not a physiological constant. It's a voluntary activity!" Oh, wait. Dase just remembered some things they had read about the primitives. Frantically, they steered towards another topic before the conversation took an ugly turn.

"Blood type! How about blood type? What are you? I'm O+. If you're really tied to the word, you can call people who are type O *women*, you can call people who are type A, or whichever one you are, *men*, and we can make up words for the other two. Of course blood type is a little more complex than that, but it's all about simplifying anyway, isn't it?

"Now, I recognize that, same as chromosomes, you can't tell what blood gender someone belongs to by looking at them, but in this case it's not actually a drawback, cause you have to do the test anyway before a blood transfusion, which is the only situation in which it's important."

"It's not..." Robert sputtered some more. "Blood type is blood type, sex is sex."

"The reflexive property, okay. You're on your way to algebra. A = A. But if A is invalid, it's not going to help you out much. You can say that anyone who doesn't shave their chin has man blood, and that's all fine, but a lot of people are going to die if you organize blood transfusions that way. Your system just doesn't hold up in the real world."

"The real world? In the real world, outside of your university campus—"

"—I didn't go to university—"

"—*he* and *she* have always existed."

"Well you know that can't be true," Dase dug in. "English has not always existed, so clearly any words that belong to English, or used to, are just a blip in history. And don't try to say all languages have *he* and *she* equivalents."

Robert set their jaw. "The concepts. Have always existed."

"Concepts? That always exist?" Dase giggled. "That would require..." Oh right. Dase remembered another thing the primitives were said to believe in. A real argument stopper. They could see that Robert was getting irate, bordering on violent, so they decided to change track.

"Look. I'll call you whatever you want. You call me what I want. We can both be happy. Good?"

Robert nodded, though their eyes still smoldered.

"Great. So what is it for you, your wife? He?"

"I'm he, she's a she."

"Great! And they for me! Though of course, when you're talking to me, 'you' works just fine," Dase managed a friendly smile. "So... now that we've had it out... What's a wife?"

———

Much to Robert's relief, they—*he*—was sent somewhere else after another day in the cell next to Dase. They had not gotten much further in their conversations. Really, each of them represented to the other an enbihess. Dase was shocked, not only by Robert's ignorance, but by his complete lack of curiosity, his inability to be challenged. Whoever ran the Secession, if there were people there who knew it was a lie, like the people who had designed *Hermetica*, they probably had a really easy job.

The transfer happened while Dase was sleeping, just as when Robert arrived. When Dase awoke, he was no longer there. They wondered if there were sedatives in the food. Did they move prisoners without witnesses to increase the sense of solitude, to reduce the information one had about the place and how it operated?

The metallic column pinged. Dase removed the tray, but rather than eating, they paced around the cell a bit. They needed music. The Moonlight Sonata came to mind, but the acoustics were terrible, the plexi and the lighting didn't help at all. They labored through a few bars, repeated them when the rest didn't come, and gave up.

In another attempt to harness their mind's wild horses, they sat down for a few rounds of crunches. Their motivation soon fizzled. They got up and ate the contents of the tray. Paced around a bit. Fell into a slumber.

When Dase awoke, there was a new person in the next cell. They were older. Dase got up and walked over to the plexi. Would this become a routine?

"Hi. I'm Dase."

"Hi Dase, I'm Shawna."

"Should I use they, he...?"

"They is fine. You go by they?"

Dase nodded, happy that Shawna didn't seem to take offense at the question.

"What storyline are you from?"

"Storyline?"

Shawna bit their lip. "What do you know?"

Dase gave a long sigh. They could tell Shawna knew more

than they did, and certainly more than Robert had. "I grew up on a ship called *Hermetica*, but it turned out we've been on Terra the whole time."

Shawna nodded sadly. "Terra, yeah. We call it Earth here."

"Right, Earth." Dase couldn't keep the bitterness out of their voice. "You asked me about storylines. What did you mean?"

Shawna looked around slowly and leaned in, their hand against the plexi. "A few decades ago, actually, it would have been right around the time you were born, things were really bad. Society was falling apart. The program was so dysfunctional, even those who benefited the most couldn't ignore it. Systems collapse at every level. Overheating. Starvation. Then there was a pandemic. Massive, deadly. Then a coup attempt. A lot of fighting. So they initiated the Compartmentalization."

"They?"

"At a certain point the government signed on, took it over. But in the beginning it was the ones who owned the technology. The idea was to separate people as much as possible. Defuse the conflict. Actually, they'd already been doing it for a long time. I guess it started out as just another marketing scheme. But it got out of control, and in the end the only solution they found was to make it total."

"Make what total? What were they doing?"

Shawna looked into Dase's eyes a long moment, weighing them, then let out a deep sigh. "Parallel worlds."

Parallel worlds? What did that mean?

"It actually goes... way back. Decades. They started selling the idea that you had to buy your identity. The clothes you wore, the music you listened to, the hobbies you had, the vacations you took, the car you drove. They sold the idea that all that stuff was the way to express who you were. And people bought it. They bought it big time. I guess it was inevitable that after buying their identity for so long, they would buy their reality."

"How... did that work?" Dase only had a loose idea about buying things, and they weren't sure if it was that or the concept of parallel worlds giving them the most trouble.

"You got to understand, by that point, 95% of people's perceptions were managed through social networking. Their news, their history, their science, even their enemies, they only chose things that fit their identity. Collectively, in groups. You could think of it as separate columns in society. They just constructed their own realities. It wasn't entirely up to them, of course, it was a managed process. Only profitable realities could be produced, because of who owned the technologies, the metrics they used.

"And at first it was just that. Streamlining the whole process of buying and selling. But it had unintended consequences. People refused to believe anything that contradicted them. When the pandemic hit, hundreds of thousands of people were dying, and one group, they just denied the entire thing. Said it wasn't happening, that it was some plot, and they tried to take over. They were attacking doctors, killing immigrants, Black people."

"Black people?"

"Oh boy." All the lines on Shawna's face deepened tenfold. "I don't know how much Earth history you read on *Hermetica*. This country... from the beginning, it was based on kidnapping people like me and forcing us to work as slaves. And then they made us call it the Land of the Free."

Dase didn't know what to do with that information. "That's... perverse."

In a flash, all the movies they had ever watched came back to them. All the ones with Terran actors, the pasty skin of the protagonists, and how all the actors with darker skin played auxiliaries or villains. Of course, the actors spoke the lines the writers fed them, but they still had to stay within the register established by all the performances recorded into the database while those actors were still alive. The AI couldn't make a movie out of whole cloth.

Seeing those performances within the blissful comfort of their module, their outrageous hijinks, their impossibly good luck, their motivations inhumanly heroic or petty, the protagonists' rare skin tones had simply amplified the exoticism of it all. In the original context, back on Terra, on Earth, was the entire purpose of those movies just to reinforce a vast and arbitrary order, to confirm the dominance and entitlement of some, and the inferiority of others?

"Yeah, it is. And some of those people? They never forgave us. For what *they* did to *us*. So I guess if we're going to be completely honest, some people have been living in parallel worlds for centuries. Maybe the whole thing was destined to fall apart from the start."

"So... they were killing you? People like you?"

"Yeah." Shawna moved their hand so it was closer to Dase's, just on the other side of the plexi. "People like you, too. I don't know your background, but if you ended up on *Hermetica*, you're not one of them. Dase... they probably killed your parents. Maybe directly, more likely through negligence. The pandemic."

"My parents?" Dase asked numbly. The thought was overwhelmingly strange. "They told me I was from an artificial insemination, from a harvested egg. Like all the others."

"*Hermetica* was one of the first storylines to develop. When the government decided to take it over and go total. It was the pilot program. There were a lot of orphans. The pandemic, the social breakdown in general. The youngest ones, they decided to give them a chance for something better.

Once it went total, the Compartmentalization I mean, every parallel world had to play a function. They had to produce something."

"Like what?"

"*Hermetica* produces scientists. Some of the best. They think they're working on the ship, improving the life support, propulsion, getting ready to terraform a new homeworld. Actually, their research agendas get fed to them from outside of *Hermetica*, based on the needs of the different agencies here on the outside. Every researcher on *Hermetica* has such a tiny window, such an extremely, hyper-specific line of inquiry and experimentation, they never know. But everything they develop is linked to some program out here. Improving energy efficiency, cleaning up the disaster, carbon sequestration, geoengineering, medical research, social surveillance and pacification."

"So. They're imprisoning us. All of us. And just using us."

"Yeah. Yeah. I'm sorry you have to find out this way."

"How do you know all this?"

Shawna looked down towards the ground, their gaze dissipating into a blank mirror. "I'm a writer."

"What?"

"I work on the storylines."

Dase didn't know whether to feel infuriated or fascinated. They held their tongue.

"I, um..." Shawna swallowed. "The systems are mostly self-managing. The different worlds, I mean. *Hermetica* was an exception, but the older people involved, the ones who educated you, they've been mostly phased out as the first cohorts reached adulthood. The other worlds, they're all held together by the subjects themselves and good programming. But to start, they needed the right stories. Most of the stories were already there, latent in the different columns I described.

The beliefs that people had arrayed around themselves to protect these identities they'd created, they already had all the elements. They just needed to be organized, given a good plot, and then they were set in motion. And we'd keep an eye on them, introduce new elements if it was needed, if people were getting bored or starting to have doubts."

"You made this."

Shawna swallowed again. "Other people made it. It was already underway when I started..."

"You helped make it. You kept it functioning. You just said so yourself."

"I wish I'd had other choices, but I needed to make a living."

"Did you write my storyline? Did you write *Hermetica*?"

"No. I got recruited for another storyline."

"What does that mean, you were recruited?"

"I didn't fit into any of the columns. There were a lot of us who were problematic for the Compartmentalization. Some of them are still out in the streets, in one of the dead zones, trying to stay alive. Most of them are gone already. Others, we got recruited."

"What did they give you?" Dase reached out for an archaic word they knew from their novels. "What did they *pay* you to do this to us?"

Shawna splayed their hands in tired resignation. "You don't have to offer much when the alternative is going hungry."

Dase nodded. They didn't know what hunger was, not personally. $x > y$, where y was Shawna's integrity and x, the price they'd offered. With no way of ascertaining the value of leaving behind hunger and uncertainty, they had to admit they had no information concerning the value of y. They let it go.

"How'd you end up here?"

"Sabotage."

Dase raised an eyebrow.

"I started putting some clues in the storyline I was overseeing. Some open-ended plot elements. I wanted them to have a chance."

Dase went and sat back down on the cot. Now they felt bad for getting angry. Dase had gotten locked up here for trying to free themself. It seemed Shawna had gotten locked up, and had possibly lost a good life, for trying to help others get free.

"Do you hate me?"

"I don't know you."

"I know you don't want to hear this, but when has it ever been any better? People see what they want to see."

Dase couldn't argue with that. They curled up and pulled the covers high, thinking about Snookums.

Another tray, another meal. Dase went back to the plexi they shared with Shawna. Graciously, Shawna rose to meet them.

"The person there before you. They—he—was from the Secession."

Shawna nodded.

"That's a pretty awful place. Did you write that one?"

"No," Shawna said vehemently. "That place was there way before I got in."

"You said *Hermetica* was the first one."

"The first one the government created. The Secession, that one got built up as soon as the technology existed. All the most profitable stories in one place."

Dase narrowed their eyes suspiciously.

"Dase, listen to me." They looked up and saw pain in Shawna's face, and realized they were being self-centered.

They felt sure then that Shawna had been through a worse hell than they ever had endured on *Hermetica*. "That place is real. Too fucking real. We didn't make that. That's on them. They were actually going around killing people. You got a sense of that, didn't you, talking to him?"

Dase nodded.

"What were we going to do with them? Put them all in one place, let them think they've won, it's the least violent solution. But what the hell am I saying? *We*. Like it was my choice, like I was in charge." Shawna banged a fist on the plexi. "That's how they do it. They get in your head. They get you to think you're a part of their *we*. *We the people*. They invite you into their shoes so you can see how perfectly reasonable all their decisions are. And it's tempting to put on their shoes when you have to go barefoot. But it's a fucking lie. I'm in here with you. Before, when I was working, we were just adding the colors to a structure that had already been built. If we stopped, they found others. There were thousands of us. We were cheaper than old pennies. We provided a service, but we never had any control."

"Who does?"

"The same ones who were in control when everything started going to hell. The same ones responsible for it going to hell in the first place. It's not a group of people, Dase. It's not some cabal. It's just whoever happened to be on top. How do you get to the top? It's the most ruthless ones, the ones willing to stab anyone in the back to get ahead. And then their children, and then their children's children, staying on top as long as they can.

"And those ruthless motherfuckers: they were encouraging the people in the Secession from the very start. Giving them everything they needed, never shattering their fragile little bubble. Why should they worry? They weren't the ones getting killed. They believed a lot of the same things as those nut jobs. They were on top because they deserved to be on top. It's nice to believe that. It's nice to have cheerleaders who become attack dogs when anyone stands up to you.

"But the denialists, they just couldn't stop killing. Their masters tightened the leash, they started to bite the hand that fed them. They couldn't tell the difference. So the government stepped in, absorbed them into the Compartmentalization, let them think they broke away. The programmers simulate a border skirmish every now and then so they stay interested. It's always a war for them. In fact, the government's original plan was for the Secession to produce mercenaries, but nowadays all that stuff is done with drones and bots, so they don't need them. They do food production, now."

"He mentioned a farm."

"Yeah. They have a simulated money economy. The modelers found out they need a simple rewards system, like training dogs. They don't seem to understand math. You have them driving tractors around all day, they bring in a hundred kilos of produce, you know how much they keep? Half a kilo. In money value, but they know the exchange rate."

"And they do it anyway?"

"You know what keeps them in line? Besides doing night watch and going on border patrol."

"What?"

"The system is rigged so that every now and then, one of them gets an insane amount of money. It's presented to them as a lottery or some insurance windfall. And that person buys a huge house, more cars than they can drive, a swimming pool. And you know what? The others stay happy."

"The others?"

"Yeah. I even checked the data. The ones who are scraping by, giving away everything they work for. Their biostats go up the most in two situations: after a skirmish at the border, and after someone in their circle wins the lottery, buys a big house. When do their stats go down? If they're the one who wins the lottery, about a month after moving in to the new house."

"Yeah, Robert seemed... pretty weird."

"Did he tell you their theory?"

"Which one?"

"They think the Earth is flat."

"No."

"Yeah, they do. They really do."

"No, that's impossible. He said they have mountains. He said he's been to the ocean."

Shawna shrugged.

"Look, I know I thought I grew up on a spaceship, but they built our blocks so we could never see the horizon. If he can climb a mountain or go to the ocean, he can literally watch things go down below the horizon."

"People see what they want to see."

"Lunar eclipses," Dase protested. "You can see the shape of the Earth!"

"They see what they want to see."

The next day, Shawna was still there. Dase was feeling introspective, but eventually their thoughts overwhelmed them. They approached the plexi. Shawna rose, too.

"I always wanted to work on the sky, when I was growing up. They told us it was a projection, you know. Designers working together with Meteorology, recreating the sky on Terra. I thought I got rejected because I wasn't good enough. I guess I just had impossible dreams."

"Yeah."

"I wonder, would I be here if I had done better?"

"What do you mean?"

"Maybe I could have lived down that failure, not getting the sky, if I'd at least gotten halfway. If I'd scored higher on the aptitudes, and gotten a more interesting work assignment. If my mind were more engaged, maybe I wouldn't have gone scratching around the corners. I've never seen what other people see, not all the time, but maybe I wouldn't have gone looking so hard."

"What was your job?"

"Palliative therapist. I gave back rubs."

Shawna sighed. "You didn't get your work assignment from the aptitudes."

"What?"

"The aptitudes are a ruse. They add a little bit of data about how you perform under stress, but the system already knew your exact capacities. Physics, biology, mechanics, calculus, emotional intelligence, social hierarchy tendencies, you name it. They were testing you since you were born. They're always testing. They're testing us right now."

Dase looked around. "So, why do the aptitudes at all? They could just tell us our work assignment is based on cumulative performance scores rather than a single test."

"The test is important," Shawna replied. "But it's not what you think. They need you to believe that your entire future, your ambitions, your integration into society, are based on one single exam. And then the day of the exam, they pop a little trick question. It's usually not in the exam itself, but something related. Different every time. On *Hermetica*, what they need to know is, are you willing to falsify information, or unsee something you have seen, when you are asked to do so."

Dase rocked back on their heels.

"Yeah, it's even more insidious than you think. For the test to work, disobeying can't come with any immediate consequences. The subject has to think that disobedience will not be immediately noticed, but presents a small risk of a lower performance score, and might therefore put their social integration, their ambitions, at risk. The people on *Hermetica* are given really powerful tools. They could quickly discover the nature of their reality if they put their minds to it. Integration, performance, had to be more important to you than the truth. So if you hesitated when you got to that trick question, even for a moment, you were out."

Dase detached, feeling estranged from the memories that washed over. "I think there might have been two tricks like that," they said slowly. "I left them both blank."

"Yeah," Shawna nodded sadly. "They also test for rebellion, likelihood of protest."

Dase let out a bitter laugh.

"I'm sorry."

"Well... I guess they had me figured out pretty well after all."

Shawna took a moment to continue. "When I was getting reassigned, after my first storyline was operational, I read up on the scripts of some of the other options. I read a lot about *Hermetica*, how it worked. I turned that one down. It didn't seem right."

"It's not right."

"No."

"Are any of them any better?"

"A lot of them aren't so cruel, or so restrictive. Most of them don't start with a big group of orphans and put them in near total confinement. But confinement is an element of all the columns."

Dase looked around at the cell. "Yeah, this place could

be on *Hermetica*." Then they had a thought. "Robert said he didn't travel much. But he could. He could move around."

Anger flashed across Shawna's face, followed by exhaustion. "The ones who are really in charge, they have a lot of sympathy for the people in the Secession. Plus those people have a lot of guns and moving them, altering their story too much, would have been costly. You got to understand, the parallel worlds, they just augmented and entrenched the inequalities that already existed in the earlier system. This isn't utopia."

"No, it's a prison."

"I won't argue with you there."

"You said they're always testing. Testing us now. How?"

"How we interact, what we say, the choices we make."

"What for?"

"They're deciding on our reassignment."

"How do they do that?"

"Me, they know by now I won't keep my mouth shut. The fact I'm spilling the beans to you just confirms it. But they also know, at the end of the day, I'll lower my head and play along. I'm valuable to them as a writer. They might put me on one of the storylines where it doesn't matter if the people know about the parallel worlds, like Robotics and Efficiency. That's a boring one, just a sprawling, city-sized campus where they focus on social engineering, mechanization, machine learning, a lot of the tech that forms the basis of the other worlds, from the tractor Robert drives to the social networks that convince people on *Hermetica* that they're on a spaceship with twelve million passengers."

"Is that your best case scenario?"

"If I get really bad scores, they'll put me in Gangland, and that's where I'll spend the rest of my life."

"Gangland? I'm afraid to ask."

Shawna's eyes burned defiantly. "Ask."

"What's Gangland?"

"Think of it as the opposite of the Secession. It's where they left people they had trouble integrating, but who were the wrong color. They corralled them in the dead zones. Ghost cities full of lead, empty factories, old trash incinerators. Cities they couldn't save from the rising sea. Lot of guns, lot of drugs, lot of trauma. No medical care, no fresh food. So yeah, the opposite of the Secession, but they have something in common. Gangland's an old one. They made it before they had their social networking technologies, before the Compartmentalization."

"What tech did they use?"

"Real estate investment, homeowners' associations. Military planes coming back from Vietnam full of heroin. Defunding treatment centers, funding prisons. Machine gun-toting cops killing revolutionaries and popping kids for possession."

"I hope they don't send you there."

"It would be the smart thing for them to do. It won't matter how many people there I tell about the other worlds. They're not stupid. They know there's other worlds, and they know they're not allowed to leave the one they're stuck in. But it's not all bad. People are resourceful. There's a lot of love there."

"I guess they can't send Robert there. I'm starting to suspect he'll get off a lot easier than either of us."

"You catch on quick. What'd he do?"

"He said he shot someone."

Shawna rolled their eyes. "They'll keep him in the Secession. Probably put him in a mine making fertilizer, tell him it's prison labor, parole him in ten, twenty years if he tests well."

Dase hesitated. "And me?"

"You're a tough one," Shawna frowned. "They need to figure out where they can make you useful, where you won't cause too much trouble. You broke out of one of the most tightly controlled storylines, but you don't have the advanced training that would make you valuable elsewhere. I bet the system's having a hard time with you."

———

The next day, Shawna was gone.

Dase looked up as they awoke. Saw the next cell was empty. Laid their head back down and tried to take deep breaths.

A while later they got up. Did some exercises. Tried to remember what the sky looked like, how it felt to sit underneath it. They wished they could play some music. They tried to recall a melody in their head, the right melody for just this moment, but nothing came. The air hummed, but it wasn't alive in here. Not like outside on the block, before a storm.

After uncounted hours, the plexi before them went opaque.

"Hello, Dase," said a voice. The cell, they presumed. "Your preliminary evaluation is complete. You may choose your next assignment."

The plexi had become a screen, projecting eight large squares. Begrudgingly, Dase stepped forward.

Each square held an image. The first one portrayed a block, just like back on *Hermetica*. As they held a finger over it, the image began to move, showing a sort of montage. The image shifted from the block to the inside of a module, a supply center, a research lab, friendly-eyed people, masks over their mouths, walking past the Green or sitting on a bench. So it was, definitively, *Hermetica*. That's when they noticed the first two squares were in a muted color, more grey, lower contrast. On *Hermetica* that always signified an inactivated button.

The second such square showed a green field and a large, stand-alone house of unusual construction. Dase put their finger over it and the image moved, showing mountains, forests, a pasty-skinned person on a huge tractor, a short line of people with steely eyes walking along a wall, carrying rifles. That must be the Secession.

So *Hermetica* and the Secession were off-limits to them. How considerate of the system to let them know. They went to the next square. It showed a group of people, smiling, laughing, working on a threedee modeler, another person grouping data sets on an aitcheff interface, a cafeteria of people laughing and talking, barely paying attention to their food, two people playing chess, another group playing volleyball. Then a large swimming pool, people swimming laps. A final cut showing a person smiling triumphantly, attention divided between a portable and a team of multi-jointed robotic arms performing some complex assembly task.

Dase went to the next square. It was a night time scene, people sitting outside, crowded together around tables in the street, laughing and drinking. Then one of them was painting on a canvas. Others were rehearsing in an orchestra. One was looking appreciatively at a holographic sculpture, hand on chin, as though forming an intelligent opinion. Others were laying in a grassy park, reading off their portables.

The next option showed a couple people in masks operating a team of bulldozers, demolishing old buildings. Dase couldn't tell if they had been ruined by war or abandonment. Another team of machines came, laying foundations for new buildings that started to grow skyward.

Dase went back to their cot, turning away from the screen. There were still three squares left, but they felt estranged, knowing each of those worlds was based on a lie, feeling sickened that they were offering them the option to join one of them.

After finding out that their entire life, they had been

deceived and exploited, how were they supposed to accept anything the system wanted to offer?

Cell spoke again. "You have six choices for possible reassignment. Take your time deciding, but until you have decided, you will not be able to move into the next stage of your rehabilitation."

Six choices. Should they feel lucky? Back on their block on *Hermetica*, there were only four choices, four ways off the block, all of them heavily controlled. Now they had six. Was that progress?

Dase didn't know what to think. The idea of being alone at the helm of a host of powerful machines, bringing great buildings toppling down, appealed to the mood they were in at the moment, but the thought of the next team coming through, erecting new buildings, and the certainty of what the masters of the world would use those new buildings for, killed the fantasy.

Sure, they actually had no idea what kind of buildings they were, they hadn't gotten to the end of the promo. But could there be any doubt? They would be buildings filled with rooms. Each room would have a limited numbers of ways out. They would be buildings filled with people. Each person locked into a story they had not written.

Dase spent the rest of the day in a lethargic agony, somewhere between restlessness and nightmare.

They woke up to the sound of a ping from the metallic column. Time passed. Eventually, they got up, retrieved the tray, ate most of its contents apathetically. Laid back down.

Some time later, they got up again. Paced around the cell.

Did push ups. Punched at the plexi. Boredom taunted them: if you do not choose, this nothingness will go on forever. They felt infuriated, trapped. The walls mocked them. There was nothing in the cell they could break.

The ping sounded again. Water or food? It seemed it was feeding time again. Dase retrieved the tray, but instead of eating, they flung the contents across the cell. Something like a semi-solid, lasagna-puree splattered across the floor. One little sealed container survived the impact. Dase picked it up. It was something vaguely like pudding. They opened it, and assiduously smeared it across the plexi screen, covering up the eight squares, the six possible futures being offered.

A hissing sound came from the duct above.

Dase awoke. Their head hurt. The cell was immaculate. There was no sign of their outburst. The screen remained. Now there were only six squares. The images representing *Hermetica* and the Secession had disappeared.

The column pinged. Dase found a cup of water within. They drank it down. They went back to sleep.

Dase had been half-awake for a long time before they finally forced their eyes all the way open and rolled out of the cot. They drank some water and crossed to the other corner to piss. Finally, letting out a long sigh, they went back to the screen.

With a bitter obedience, they put a finger to the fourth square.

The image was of a beautiful white building on a cliff, with a majestic staircase winding down to a sandy beach on an azure sea. People arrived in resplendent vehicles, people evincing confidence, charm, and power. The video, however, focused on those attending them, bringing them to their rooms, cooking and serving their food, massaging them—Dase was surprised to see them use their hands directly, and not any machines—fitting them into scuba gear on the back of a small boat. The attendants were also elegant, always smiling, always right on time, in the perfect place, in a carefully choreographed dance. The guests seemed very appreciative, one even shared a bottle of wine with an attendant on the edge of a hot tub.

Dase looked back at the cell, raising an eyebrow. Being tracked was always insulting, they realized, thinking back to the aptitudes. But when the system read you so wrong, the insult seemed even worse. Then again, they had no way of knowing if the option had not been placed on the screen to elicit exactly that reaction, to push them to another choice, or at least to inflate the feeling of how many choices were available.

Could one even speak of choice? Surely the system had already calculated the probability of every possible choice. On the whole menu, there were probably only two that Dase might feasibly choose. Maybe even that calculation was optimistic. Perhaps the modeling was so exact, that everything from the mood and the lighting in the promos to the order the options were presented in were all designed to produce a single outcome. Which scenario had the system determined Dase could fit into best?

They moved their finger, if only to stop the parade of luxury and its servile attendants.

The next image was quite the contrast. A forest, ancient trees. Three people trekked through. They were tired, dirty, but there was strength in their eyes. They seemed like friends. One of them stopped, excited. They had seen something. The others gathered around. It was a moss growing at the base of the tree. They knelt down reverently, and one carefully scooped a sample into a small, self-sealing bag. Later they were at a small station, it seemed to be in the middle of the same forest. They were running tests. One of them seemed to be giving first aid to a small amphibian, a variety Dase had never seen before. The animal seemed to have some transparent, oily substance on its skin. It was suffering, but the person tended it lovingly, cleaning it off, giving it an injection with a tiny needle. Later, they were gathered around a pond, releasing the amphibian, now healthy. It swam out into the water, joining others like it.

The final square showed an angry crowd in a street, perhaps a protest. Dase did not tap on the image. They let their hand drop to their side as a deep sigh escaped their lungs. They turned and sat down on the cot.

Six options. Six possible futures. One, they had not yet seen. Another, they definitely did not want. Two of them were appealing, but they only seemed tenable for those times when they were on the up. And when would they possibly be feeling like that again, after all they had been through, after what they had to do now?

The other two, they might work. They could imagine choosing a life like that.

But no, they realized angrily. It wasn't their choice. None of those lives would ever be their choice. And then they realized why they had never been allowed to see anyone who worked in this prison, not even a simple robot. With no one else here, no one who held authority over them, the place was merely a circumstance, a fork in the road and not a prison, not a box someone had decided to lock them up inside. All of it reinforced the illusion of choice, as though they were in dialogue with those six options on the screen. As though they were about to choose their future life.

But those worlds, and all the worlds, were like the prison itself: totally designed by those who had control, completely inoculated against any choices they might make. The fact that they were invisible, the illusion that Dase could control how they lived, only augmented the architects' power.

Looking back at the plexi, Dase thought about the button that had portrayed *Hermetica*. It had initially been presented as inactivated, and then removed entirely. At first that had made perfect sense. Why should they want to return to *Hermetica*, where they had been so unhappy? Everything about it was a lie.

But then they reconsidered. That was their home. The place they had grown up. Everyone they knew was there still. What right did those in charge have to remove Dase? With a wave of disgust that hit like nausea, they realized the arrogance of it all: the Compartmentalization, the pretension of designing a world for them to live in, circumscribing their futures but always in the guise of offering them choices. If humans could go uninvited to another star system, why couldn't they go anywhere they pleased on their own planet? And who had the authority to keep Dase from going home? They had no idea who the architects were, but they certainly didn't live on Dase's block. And to whom did a block belong, if not to those who lived on it? Did they think they just owned everything?

No. Suddenly it was clear what they wanted. Dase banged on the plexi.

"*Hermetica!* I want you to send me back to *Hermetica!*" they yelled at the cell with growing conviction.

Hermetica was hell, and that was why Dase had to go back.

Zimp, Milty, even Axa, they were all trapped there, trapped in the lie. None of them deserved that, and Dase didn't deserve to be torn away from them. Even though they had spent so much of their life in solitude. But even the shrubs and flowers on the Green had been their companions. And the sky.

They banged again on the plexi. "Let me go back to *Hermetica!*"

Was Snookums still there? It didn't seem like the cat would be able to find Dase here. They started banging harder. They would go back. They would find their old friends. It wouldn't be perfect. The loneliness, the old anxieties, they would be waiting for them too. But they would tell them. And together they would change things.

Could it be possible? Would the system let them go back? Shawna had said the system was set up for everyone to be productive in some way, and the purpose of *Hermetica* was to produce scientists. Surely the passengers would still be productive even if they knew the truth. Dase couldn't imagine that Zimp would ever give up teaching quantum mechanics. The others, too, would continue with their pursuits. Only, they would do it on their own terms. They would get to decide what was useful or necessary, once they were actually allowed to know the world they lived in. Could the system countenance such a modification? Would it deign to engage in dialogue with its subjects?

Of course, Dase knew that all cybernetics entailed dialogue, and machine learning itself was based on seeking out maximum inputs. But there was another factor that had always been there, beneath the endless circuits of conversation, the socials, the peer-revieweds, the near infinite data that circulated on *Hermetica*. Even now, the entire system was seated just across the plexi from Dase. The cell itself constituted a dialogue. One that Dase had no role in shaping.

They had been taught that science was freedom: the freedom to explore, to advance any argument, tied with a responsibility to test those arguments and to consider any criticism. The examples of Terran lit they had been given to read in primary school often centered protagonists who burned with the desire to say what they really believed. Basic history from Terra was full of the same theme, like the heroic contests between Socrates and the city, or between Galileo and the Church. In a flash, Dase realized the inputs they had been given as children steered them all towards a pre-selected conclusion. Just as the Church had lulled its followers into a new prison by warning them of the dangers of idols and god kings, *Hermetica* had frightened them with tales of irrationality or excess and given them the blinders so they could move more efficiently along the one dimensional path they had been assured was the best one.

The social technologies that linked freedom with expression had become obsolete a century ago, if indeed they were ever real. Thinking furiously, Dase contrasted what they knew of the Old World, the world of Edna and Galileo, with what they knew of cybernetics. The true test to distinguish between a free system and a totalitarian system, they realized, had nothing to do with expression. On the contrary, totalitarian systems were now based on free expression, as much of it as possible. The real test was not communication, but action and influence.

Grasping for some way to make sense of it all, a model that might interpret these disparate data, Dase thought back to programming classes from before the aptitudes. In programmatic terms, are all elements enabled to rewrite code? That could be the mark of a free system, Dase supposed. When you write a program to scan for content in the library, or to tell the block when to water the flowers on the Green, you're assuming that the books don't have their own lines they would rather share, that you know better than the flowers how much water they need.

Scale up to a system full of people, a system like *Hermetica*, and now programmers are scanning people for specific content, deciding how to feed and water them, as though the programmers, and not the objects of their program, know best. Dase got a visit from a Safety investigator because some of their behaviors tripped a security program Dase was not even aware of. Module's recommendations for Dase regarding medication, diet, entertainment, and all the rest were based on other programs Dase had had no hand in crafting. Dase might be invited to evaluate the program, to rate it—and in fact Module constantly sought out feedback from Dase in the form of biostats and cognitive indicators—but they never had authorship over it. While the program's parameters surely aimed to ensure Dase's health, it was clear that a more fundamental parameter was the security of the overall system, the continued operation of central programming.

If they were free, according to this rudimentary definition, if they could reprogram the program they were caught up in, the elements on *Hermetica*, the people, would mostly want to continue their research. Dase was sure of it. After all, one of the things that had set them apart was that unlike the rest of their cohort, they did not feel fulfilled by their work. Nearly everyone else did. And if they could, the others would want to redesign the work, modify its objectives and parameters. If, instead of being trapped in a lie, they were allowed to dialogue with other elements of the Earth system, formulating their own needs and requests pertaining to scientific research, they might arrive at shared sets of objectives and parameters. That's what a free system looked like. It didn't mean you were free of consequences or free of the need to compromise, but that every step of the way, you had a hand in shaping outcomes and that you could refuse a collaboration that was contrary to your interests.

Surely that was a viable parameter? Dase felt breathless, wondered if Galileo had had a moment like this one.

Their mind raced ahead. How does this thing, this "free system," as they were venturing to call it, compare to its Other? Perhaps the question posed an overly binary lens, but it was a useful one for now. So if *Hermetica*—or the whole world, as seemed to be the case—were not a free system, but a totalitarian system, what defined it as such?

A totalitarian system, Dase felt confident in their hunch, would encourage input from all elements. But where would those inputs go? Not to the elements themselves. Need To Know, the New Safety, *trust the experts, Remember the Wiki*, as well as the parallel worlds Shawna had described, all these data seemed to point to the same fact. Only those with an exclusive administrative access would be able to analyze the inputs and decide how to act on them. Of the system's total code, a large proportion would be fundamental protocols that the vast majority of elements would have no ability to alter. Again, alterations would be the prerogative of admin. Sure, some portion of the code could be modified by everyday elements with something like a "guest" or "user" level access, but the changes would be largely cosmetic, and the parameters for those changes would be limited in advance by admin. In the end, it didn't even matter who got to be admin, so long as most people were just guests in their own system.

So, if Dase were allowed to go back, if the people on *Hermetica* could get free, it wouldn't mean the end of existence for whomever was in control. It simply meant they would have to shift from relations of command to relations of reciprocity. Were they up for the change?

What could Dase do but insist? They went back to banging. Their fist was bruising.

Finally, Cell recognized that ignoring Dase was no longer the best option. Which metric had been tripped to change its stance? Physical damage to Dase's body? Damage to the cell? Were there other people farther down the corridor who might hear?

Before Dase could consider what options for action these different possibilities might present—a damage-prone plexi, a cell coded to protect their bodily integrity, other prisoners with whom they might communicate—the plexi phased back into a screen. This time, only one item appeared, though it was huge and took up half the wall. A little unsubtle: it was the icon for the *Hermetica* button, in inactivated grey scale, situated inside a giant red circle and with a diagonal red line crossing it out for good measure.

"*Hermetica* is not an option. You have 0% chance of being reassigned to *Hermetica*. You have six options, and must choose one of them before moving on to the next stage of your rehabilitation. This is your last warning to cease attempted destructive activity of the structures of this cell."

Now Dase slammed both fists into the plexi, again and again, followed by a series of frontal kicks. "You motherfuckers!" they screamed, taking the insult Shawna had used. "You kidnapping motherfuckers! Send me home! Fuck your six choices, send me home!" They were crying now. "That's my family! Give me my family back, you motherfuckers!"

A hissing sound came from the duct above.

———

Dase awoke. Their head hurt. The plexi was intact. Six squares glowed softly in its center. There would be no dialogue. Whatever Dase might want or need was completely irrelevant. They were a machine to be programmed. They stayed a long time in bed.

What would Shawna do, they wondered, crawling out of a sordid dream. If they were a writer, Dase could think of a fantastical ending to this story. They would choose one of the options Cell offered them. They would explore their new world. Make friends. Together they would find a crack in the system. Escape. Out into the real world. And live happily ever after. Or at least, the story would end ambiguously, with all the possibilities of the new world left unexplored, readers encouraged to hope for the best. Another closed system bounded by the complicity of spectators who violated the first law of thermodynamics, creating something out of nothing, summoning hope and possibility out of a history that offered neither.

They were in an eternal present, Dase realized. There were no cracks, there was no outside the system, there was no real world apart from this one. The unseen, what they could not know from their present vantage, that *terra incognita* in which they safely stashed their neuroses about a better world, it wasn't an outside, and it certainly wasn't a whole world. The only shadows of possibility lay behind another enclosure. It was the darkness within a closed box, bounded and contained, and inside, nothing but Schrödinger's cat. Within that darkness, that uncertainty, Dase might imagine a whole world of possibilities, but really there were only two: the cat was either dead, or trapped within the box. Death or imprisonment. There were no other possibilities. Dase would not tell themself lies.

Dase drifted in and out of sleep. The column pinged, there were pings in their dreams. How many times? They did not get up. They stayed in bed until their body ached, stayed until it was past aching, stayed until their dreams went on strike and sleep refused to rescue them.

They got up, went to the toilet. The pain in their midsection began to subside. They drank some water from the column. The pain in their throat began to subside. They paced back and forth a few times, felt their blood flow, their mind come awake.

Something whispered back there. It was like a pressure, a little package begging to be opened. The column pinged again, and the thought was lost.

It was clear, now. They would keep them in here until they chose. There were six options, and that was all. They were prepared to feed them, to keep them alive indefinitely, a sort of suspended animation, until they agreed to one of those six futures. And that consent would be their first form of participation. From then on, all their actions would be modulated to improve their life within the bounds the architects had set.

When would an opportunity ever arise for something different? When could they possibly hope to be in a situation where they had more leverage than those in charge?

A simple thought popped into their mind.

If not now, when?

The whisper at the back of their mind returned, and they repeated the question: if not now, when? The pressure grew, the shape revealed itself, and as Dase let it unfold, it came through with the sudden force of violins in crescendo. It was a song, the song they had been trying to summon for the last few days. It was Vivaldi's Concerto No. 2 in G Minor, *L'Estate*, Presto.

And it thundered from their mind and throughout their very being, out their fingertips and from their feet into the floor. The walls of the cell shook with the song. Cell was not entirely immune to life, either. And Dase remembered another storm, and the most important lesson of all.

There are always other choices. There is always another way out.

And then they saw the opportunity. They saw the exact point where they had more leverage than those, great and invisible, who built entire worlds.

Knowing Cell was watching, knowing their gesture mattered whether it had an audience or not, because it was an action that struck at the very nexus where all the system's powers came to a focus, Dase got up. They walked to the column and opened it. They took out the tray of food.

There it was. The next meal, the bland mash of calories and vitamins that would keep them in this state of suspended animation until they made a choice, one of the choices the system offered, another world, identical to this one in all but appearance.

Would they have the strength to make this choice, their own choice?

They trembled. Frozen to the spot, they doubted. Then they turned. One foot in front of the other, they crossed to the toilet. Dase didn't know if they would have the strength to follow their plan to the bitter end. They didn't know what their jailers would do to try to stop them. They were in uncharted territory. And that meant, they were free already.

Dase upended the tray, dumping all the food into the shallow bowl of the toilet. Still trembling, they returned the tray to the column, closed the little door, and sat back down on the cot. There would be no suspended animation, no slowly wearing them down until they chose a world immune to their touch. Over this, their own self, they had more leverage than the architects ever could.

They had made their move. They would refuse every one of the offered choices. They were breaking out.

The storm thundered and crashed all around, but within, Dase was tranquil, calm, ready for what might come.

3

DASE LAY ON THE COT, HUGGING THEIR KNEES TO their chest. The pangs had left them some time ago. Now their body felt warm and light. They were on their way. The cell came and went. They had seen Zimp, Milty, had called out to them, but their friends couldn't hear, not yet. Snookums had visited, though Dase couldn't remember if that had been in the cell or back on *Hermetica*. It was a joyful reunion.

They'll be coming for me soon, Dase thought to themself. They had supposed from the start they wouldn't be allowed to just waste away. The jailers, whoever they were, could resort to force feeding. But at least then they would have to appear. To abandon their conceit that this was a circumstance, and not a prison. One that they built and maintained. Dase could count that as a victory, and no small one.

A shudder passed through their body. It came with the force of catastrophe, like the whole world were shaking. Dase found themself panting as it subsided. They let out a long, trembling sigh, but still their heart raced. They were stretched out now. They rubbed their arms, embracing themself.

"You did alright."

If they didn't give themself love, who would?

It had been a hard life. Not the one they'd wanted. So little to look back on. But as the light trembled and sputtered, malnourished, disbelieved, Dase felt another life ready to open like a flower and draw them in. They imagined trumpets blowing and towers falling and they smiled at the thought.

"You did alright." Barely a whisper.

Everything was warmth. No one would remember them, but it was okay. Dase had never wanted recognition. They would never be a hero. The neighbors from their block, practical people, they would disparage Dase's sacrifice if they knew, or at least try to dissuade them. Their world could not hold itself up if Dase were right. Their labyrinths were longer to run, but it didn't matter. There were no winners here.

Footsteps seemed to echo in the corridor. It didn't matter. Dase doubted anyone could overcome their simple decision. They smiled. Let them try. None of it mattered. Everything was warmth.

Dase could hear it now. Not the corridor. Not the cell. The music behind the music. They'd felt it there their entire life and now it sounded clearly. The colors, the sounds, everywhere, in everything. Dase smiled, Dase cried. They were on their way.

The stories we tell matter. The stories that the dominant culture tells us are intended to perpetuate that culture. We intend to tell stories that will end that culture.

More fiction from Detritus Books:

DARLINGTONIA
Alba Roja

"Not the day after tomorrow, not a near-future dystopia; Darlingtonia is a novel of the world right outside your own window. Don't talk about it on social media; don't text about it. Buy hard copies and hand them out to strangers."

    —Nick Mamatas, author of *Sensation* and *I Am Providence*

"Like hiding a magical hallucinogen by rolling it into a regular looking cigarette, the Alba Roja collective has passed us something radical by concealing it within a familiar form. Darlingtonia presents a hopeful story of awakening within our current dystopic reality. It asserts the possibility that our sexuality and our hunger, our creativity and our restlessness can turn in an instant, into revolutionary weapons.

Illicit and thrilling, this is a consciousness expanding, euphoria inducing novel. I loved it."

    –Joni Murphy, author of *Double Teenage*

Alba Roja is an anonymous collective of individuals strewn along the West Coast of the United States.

detritus books

Available from Detritus Books
ISBN: 978-0939306138
Distributed by AK Press
334 pages; $16.00
detritusbooks.com

SECOLO NUOVO
FULVIA FERRARI

A story of witches, anarchists, gnostics, indigenous outlaws, bandits, heretics, sunflowers, sailors, lavender, salmon, longshoremen, bank robbers, dynamiters, country farmers, alchemists, crimps, pimps, brothels, oceans, alembics, maroon colonies, mad scientists, artists, boats, depraved capitalists, grapes, cooks, vigilantes, teamsters, horses, libraries, traitors to the nation, hobos, miners, dancing, guerrilla leaders, mountains, religious movements, crumbling empires, nihilists, wagons, armed uprisings, wine, revolutionaries, peasants, military defectors, books, and the wireless transmission of electric energy.

detritus books

Published by Detritus Books
ISBN: 978-1948501149
Distributed by AK Press
470 pages; $20.00
detritusbooks.com